SNOWY

The Story of an Egret

SNOWY

The Story of an Egret

by
GRIFFING BANCROFT

Illustrations by Mel Hunter

The McCall Publishing Company
NEW YORK

The McCall Publishing Company
230 Park Avenue
New York, N.Y. 10017

*To Margaret W. Bancroft and to the
memory of her husband and my father*

At a distance the Key looks like hundreds of other small mangrove islands that dot the inland waters of southwest Florida. Once there had been nothing there, an expanse of water between the mainland and the chain of larger islands sweeping out into the gulf. Then a seed, dropped from a red mangrove tree, came floating out from the mainland a mile and a half away.

It was a seed with a long tail. Where the water shallowed, it struck the muddy bottom, held, and took root. As a new tree grew, roots sprang out from its branches in the air, reaching downward. Soon more trees sprouted, and there developed a tangled mass of roots and trunks, stems and branches.

Silt and sand carried by the tides were trapped and stopped. Solid earth began forming behind the mangroves. This killed the trees since red mangrove roots demand air and water, not earth. Thus the Key took its present form: an irregular circle of red mangroves, a tangle reaching ever outward for air and open water, and within the circle earth and sand had eliminated the original growth.

But on this earth and sand other seeds had come, carried by the winds or tides or birds. Other plants had sprung up: white mangroves and buttonwood trees, cacti, cabbage palms, a few big gumbo limbo trees, and *a dense assortment of shrubs and bushes. In all, the Key made up about three acres, half of it the circle of red mangroves over the water, half the solid land with its varied vegetation.*

Fishermen out in the deeper water, those fishing for a living or those fishing for pleasure, would scarcely notice the Key. Only when you came closer could you see that it had inhabitants. Except that some of the trees were whitened and some had dying limbs the Key blended into the mangroves of the shore.

Passengers in the big airliners that often passed overhead would not notice the Key at all, a tiny speck among many on the waters below. They would be too busy getting ready to deplane and go about their businesses or vacations, too absorbed in their own world to be aware of this world below them.

Only rarely would men come to the Key. Sometimes men with serious purpose; sometimes marauding men, vandals breaking their own laws. For the Key was not of the world of men, the current Lords of the Earth with power to change their world. This was a different world, unchangeable by its inhabitants, but an older and wiser world, governed by its own laws, older, time-tested laws.

Here was a world where species co-existed with species, where killing was only for survival, where a lasting balance had been struck between predator and prey. This was the world of the hero of this tale.

SNOWY

The Story of an Egret

I

His first sensation was one that would be part of almost all his waking hours from now on: hunger. The first sound that he heard was a frightening cacophony of *kuks* and *arks* and *caws* all about him. The first thing that he saw, as his eyes struggled open, was a glistening white figure towering over him, shading him.

Somehow he knew his survival depended on this figure, that it would appease his hunger, protect him from the unknown terrors around him. He was too weak to move. He lay on the twigs and leaves and watched.

After a time the white figure above him cried out

and moved aside. He heard another cry above the continuous din around him, a swish of air, and another, similar white figure appeared within his view. The two bowed to each other. There was a dazzling display of gleaming plumes, the white contrasting sharply with the black beaks and legs and golden yellow feet. Beaks and necks were rubbed together.

He felt a gnawing impatience with all this and tried to move, to cry. But then he heard loud sounds close at hand: *kek-kek-kek!* It was another little one, like himself but larger, bumping against him and expressing his impatience more audibly. It was a brother, two days older, who now began to show his annoyance even more forcefully, lunging at the newly arrived parent.

The smaller one longed to join in this attack. He sensed its purpose had something to do with the hollow hunger growing inside him. He tried to raise his head but it was much too heavy. He could only lie there watching his brother's continued pecking at whatever part of his parent he could reach, demanding an appeasement of his hunger.

The parent stood on the edge of the nest. He appeared indifferent but he was not. The cries and pecking of the youngster released within him a desire to offer food. He looked down at his offspring. There were four. One was just emerging from the egg, bits of shell still clinging to his damp, nearly naked body; the next was the one just achieving his awareness of things, now dry and partly covered with white down; the third was a sister a day older but still almost as helpless; the fourth was the first-hatched brother, the one lunging and crying lustily.

The father longed to give his little ones their food

but he knew he must wait. The flight back from the mud flats had not taken long; the ceremonial greeting as he relieved his mate so she could go off for food had taken only a few moments. Later he could feed these babies half-digested matter, but now the little stomachs could handle only soft, almost liquid diets.

True, he had searched for the softest foods he could find—tiny baby shrimp, insect larvae, worms—but digestion had only started. So, father stood stolidly, enduring the pecking of his legs and underparts, while he let his stomach do its work. But his digestive juices were strong and soon the food was ready. He turned his long neck down toward the youngsters. The pecking and the crying stopped. Eager little beaks flew open.

The parental beak went into that of the older brother first and that little one greedily gulped down the moist warm offering. As this was going on the sister had managed to raise her head a little and was now crying *kek-kek-kek*, begging for food. The father finally shook the older one off and put his long slender beak into that of his daughter.

The next younger brother, Snowy we shall call him, watched, his own hunger increasing at the sight of others being fed. He still could not raise his head, but now he did manage a few feeble squawks registering his displeasure. His father paid no attention. The two-day-old baby's body was still fat from the nourishment of the egg. It would be another day before he really needed food.

The next day Snowy did manage to get one of the feedings. The older brother, stronger now, expressed his eagerness and impatience by actually grasping the parental beak in his own little one and shaking it. He was rewarded with the first helping, but the parent, this time it was the mother, then turned to the sister, who was squawking lustily, and finally to Snowy, who could just manage to get his head up and beak open. And this time it was the little brother, the fourth baby, who lay in helpless frustration.

Soon all the youngsters were being fed. Each feeding was a contest in strength and guile in which the older ones tended to get the most. When a parent returned with a stomach full, all the youngsters started screaming at him and at each other. Struggling and shoving, they fought for positions nearest the old bird and, whenever it could be reached, one of them would seize the parent's bill and shake it as hard as he could.

Snowy had two siblings older and larger than he. Against this competition he had to be wily if he was going to get his share. And he was. It was a matter of timing. He noticed that one parent was always on guard, on the edge of the nest or perching nearby. When the other returned from the feeding grounds, there was always the ceremonious greeting, the bowing and glistening display of white plumes, the rubbing of bills and necks.

Snowy learned when this was about to end. He waited and saved his strength while his brother and sister fought for strategic posts at the edge of the nest. Then, if he timed things just right, he often managed to slip his gaping beak up between them and get fed before the supply ran out.

But what of baby brother, the youngest? Against the three older ones he did not have much chance. He could only squawk weakly for food in his agonizing hunger; he didn't get much. It was almost always gone before the parent managed to shake off the others and get to him.

The reason for this was, of course, way beyond his understanding or that of his parents. There were many visible enemies around the Key that could be seen and understood, and guarding their young from these and securing food occupied all the parents' time. They did not know that their greatest danger was remote, unseen.

Had there been food enough, all four babies could have been raised. Indeed, in past years sometimes five were raised. But now food was getting scarcer. Some birds in the colony simply laid fewer eggs when food was scarce, sets of three or even two. For now many of the nearby tidal flats and the marshes where the food must come from had disappeared. They had been drained and filled, and the teeming aquatic life had been replaced by housing for the current Lords of the Earth.

Try as the parents did, with continuous trips to and from the feeding grounds, they simply could not secure food enough for all. Snowy and the older ones left none for baby brother. Slowly he wasted away until one day his feeble squawking stopped altogether.

It had been, as a matter of fact, a particularly long time between feedings and all the youngsters were ravenous. They pecked at the twigs and branches that formed their home, and stabbed their sharp bills at each other. The older brother pecked at the little one and found there was no response. He seized the lifeless little baby and got its head into his mouth.

Snowy and his sister caught the idea at once. She seized the tiny feet while Snowy got his beak around the upper legs. Thus they struggled over the body of their brother. But Snowy's guile was of no avail here. He was soon shaken off. The two older ones tugged and pulled but, with bulging neck, it was the older and stronger brother who finally got the head down and forced the sister to let go.

He then lay back, stuffed, waiting for the head to be digested so the cannibalism could be completed. The parent, standing guard as always beside the nest, looked on with apparent unconcern. After all, the dead must serve the living.

Snowy, who had lost out in this struggle over his brother's body, won out in the end. For, when the parent returned with food, his competitors were so exhausted they could only lie panting while Snowy had the entire feeding to himself.

It was the first time Snowy had been fed enough so his gnawing hunger would allow him to take some note of the world around him.

He was familiar with his immediate surroundings. The nest was a rather flimsy platform not much more than a foot across, just large enough to contain the young-sters. But as the babies grew, the parents enlarged it a little by adding sticks from time to time.

This also built up the rim somewhat and afforded more protection against one of them falling out—a constant danger since the concavity of the nest was slight. The mangrove leaves which had served as lining had by now turned brown, and many had been pushed out so the floor consisted mainly of the interlaced twigs.

The nest was ten feet up, near the top of a red man-grove. It was on the inner edge of the circle of these trees, just over dry ground. Out toward the water were other red mangroves and inland, on the earth and sand, were other trees, bushes, and plants. It was higher than most of the other small heron nests, so Snowy could see a little more of the world about him.

It was a world of confusion that verged on madness. Snowy could see nests in every tree and bush, nests ranging in size from his small one to the huge platforms of the *Great Blue Herons,* three or four feet across.

The process of bringing on the new generation was in every stage. Some nests were empty with birds standing guard waiting to lay their eggs. Some had birds setting down low, incubating eggs. Many young birds, older than Snowy, were clinging to limbs and branches outside their nests. Most of the nests, even of different kinds of birds, were within a few feet of each other. In his own tree, Snowy could see nests below, above, and on either side of him.

Snowy's eyesight was acute, and from now on he would be aware of constant movement and flashing colors as birds came and went on their housekeeping duties: gleaming whites like his parents, blues and blacks, browns and bronzes, grays and multicolors of other birds. His was a colorful world.

His hearing was also acute, and the din was incessant. But soon he would be able to pick out individual cries from the unremitting babble and fit the sounds to different birds and give them meaning: cries of warning and alarm, of hunger and love, of fear and anger. He would learn to recognize the commands of his parents and the belligerent notes of his nest mates. His was a noisy world.

His sense of smell, however, was rudimentary. So he was spared at least that dimension of the confusion in which he found himself. For, to mammalian olfactory equipment, at least, his was also a smelly world.

Slowly, Snowy began to differentiate between the

birds around him. Many were little *Egrets*, or *White Herons*, like himself. He soon learned to tell his parents from the others and to recognize the cry of a parent, especially when it heralded incoming food. At other times he often watched the other egrets coming into and leaving their nests.

Always there was a call from the approaching bird which released a friendly response from the mate, and a ceremony of mutual affection would take place. There was, however, a great deal of individual variation in this. Some, like Snowy's parents, spent several minutes bowing, displaying plumes and rubbing bills and necks. Others were satisfied with only a perfunctory bow and display.

Still others made even more of a fuss over each other. On one nearby nest a little egret, somewhat behind Snowy's parents, was still setting on her eggs. Whenever she heard the soft *coo-coo-coo* of her approaching mate she would rise up, spread her plumes in welcome, and give an answering cry. He would land on the branch a few feet from the nest, spreading his plumes to the fullest, and advance with solemn bows. Finally he would lay his neck across hers and gently caress her.

She would then leave for the feeding grounds, and he would take his turn, spreading his breast feathers and pressing his warm, dark flesh to the eggs. When she came back she would often gently nudge him to get off the eggs so she could take her turn. At such times he would sometimes go out and find a stick—often pilfering it from another nest—and, bowing gracefully, proffer it to her. She would take it and weave it into the nest before resuming the setting.

The owner of the stolen stick, if aware of the theft,

would protest loudly and seek to get it back. So, while on the whole the different birds in the colony got along well together, there were sometimes squabbles. Sometimes, in fact, eggs were rolled out of nests, shaken, as birds fought over a twig.

Snowy's nearest neighbors in a nest five feet away, were young birds about the same age and size as himself. Like him they were covered with pure white down and seemed to be of his kind. But he noticed that the parent bird, standing guard as his parents did, was not white but a delicate deep blue with a trace of rustiness in the plumes along the upper neck and head. These were *Little Blue Herons*, whose young would be white like Snowy for the first year of their lives. The little babies were about the most pugnacious of the small herons, constantly clamoring and fighting each other for food.

There was one other close cousin of Snowy's, another little heron. He saw quite a few of them, rather noisy birds, all blue except for gleaming white breasts and a white plume on the head. These were *Louisiana Herons*, and their downy babies were colored just like the old birds: dark on top and light underneath. These herons were perhaps the most affectionate of all, often spending long periods perched together, preening each other's feathers.

Like most things the birds did, the greetings and affectionate displays served a purpose. They were an important aid to survival in a crowded colony. In the first place they served to strengthen the pair bond, the relationship formulated in courtship and mating. It was essential that this bond be maintained if young were to be raised, for from its earliest beginnings the nest had to be guarded constantly, and this required two birds working in relays. The nest relief ceremonies were also a form of communication necessary to insure recognition of a mate or a parent in order that a friendly response would be released to the proper individual. The neglect of these ceremonies could often cause trouble as Snowy was to find out.

One day he heard some shrieking cries that rose above even the usual din of the colony. They came from a nest in a bush near the middle of the Key. A big bird, quite unlike his parents, a stockier bird, grayish instead of white with a black cap and long white plume feathers and the largest eyes Snowy had ever seen, had landed on his nest. He had failed properly to signify his arrival, and instead of the low *coos* and eager cries from the young which usually heralded the return of a father, he was being greeted with shrieks of wrath from both his mate and the youngsters. The older birds, in fact, jabbed at each other viciously while the dark, downy young joined in a general melee. It was some time before peace was restored.

Snowy would hear quite a bit of this as time went on and sometimes would be disturbed by it in the middle of the night. For these birds were often astir in the dark. They were *Black-Crowned Night Herons* of which, fortunately, there were only a few in the colony. For they were notorious for their family quarrels.

The night herons were also cousins of Snowy, although more distant than the little herons. He also had in the colony some other heron cousins: the *American Egrets*, all white like Snowy's parents but much larger, and the even bigger, aloof, almost disdainful great blue herons, and one of these was all white, a *Great White Heron*, mate of a great blue. But in addition to these cousins, Snowy could see about him other creatures which seemed to bear little relationship to his kind except that they also had feathers and could fly.

There were a great number of black, short-legged birds whose nests were clustered together, high up in whitewashed trees. The parents kept constantly talking to their young: *arrump . . aarump . . arrump!* The young were of different sizes. Some were tiny, naked babies who sipped their regurgitated food from the parent's bill; others, larger and covered with black down, would plunge their heads almost clear down into the parent's gullet in their eagerness for food.

These were *Cormorants*. Near them were a few of their close cousins, the *Anhingas*, also darkish birds but with longer, snakelike necks. When one of the parent anhingas returned with food, the downy, buff-colored youngsters would jump up and down in excited anticipation. But the old bird, with admonishing *ka-ka-kas!*, would weave its long neck around so as to get to the smallest baby first. Then he would stretch out the neck so the baby could reach down it to get food. And, despite resistance, this one would soon be shaken off so the others could be fed in like manner.

On the outer edges of the colony, in mangroves over the water, Snowy could make out creatures of an entirely different sort, great brownish birds with buff or white necks and heads, squat and fat with long thick beaks from which hung voluminous pouches. These were *Pelicans*. When an old one returned with his pouch full of nourishment, two greedy youngsters at once would immerse their heads into it. In fact, the older young pelicans were climbing about the trees attempting to get their heads into the pouches of their neighbor's parents. Obviously many lively fights resulted from this. The old birds seldom uttered a sound, but the young pelicans were about the noisiest inhabitants of the Key.

All this and more was going on around Snowy but for the most part he paid it little heed. He had quite enough to do with his own business which was, quite simply, just keeping alive. The odds were against him. Of his generation, only one in four would live out the year. Those who made the first year would then have somewhat better chances, only a quarter of them succumbing each year thereafter. If Snowy were exceptionally canny —and lucky—he could live for almost twenty years. But it would take some doing.

Not only was there the constant problem of getting enough food, Snowy also had many active enemies who wanted only to make food of him. His first experience with one of these came when he was only a few days old.

II

Snowy's head was still big and heavy, difficult for un-
developed neck muscles to support. So it was his custom
after a feeding to lie with his head resting on the side of
the nest. In this position he would doze, although some
inner prompting always told him when a parent was
returning with food. He would be instantly awake,
clamoring with the others for his share.

One midmorning, however, he was awakened in another way. First he heard a cry from a nearby nest.
Awrk . . awrk . . awrk! Although he didn't understand,
somehow it released within him a feeling of alarm. But

his mother, who was standing guard, did understand. He felt her yellow feet go over him and saw them grasping the edge of the nest in front of him.

Then came another, different cry. And this one filled him with terror. It was a raucous *cuh . . cuh . . cuh!* Snowy and the other babies started up. He was thankful now that one of his parents was always stationed nearby. For darting in and out at his mother were three of the ugliest birds he had ever seen.

Of frightening blackness, cawing constantly, they carried on the attack. Snowy and his nest mates, trembling in panic, huddled against the far side of the nest. Their mother, plumes of neck and head and feathers bristling in anger, was warding off the attackers with her long sharp bill. Soon other herons joined in harassing the common enemy.

They were *Fish Crows,* and Snowy was destined to see a lot of their kind. Usually they would not dare molest an adult heron, but they preyed constantly on the rookeries, seeking eggs and young. Always they were there, lurking on the sidelines ready to swoop down on an unguarded nest. Occasionally, as in this instance, hunger would overcome fear and they would seek to snatch an egg or nestling even when an old bird was nearby.

The youngsters watched the combat in a mortal terror they would never forget and never entirely lose. But the crows had far too much respect for the daggerlike heron bills to try to force their way to the babies now that surprise had failed. Finally they were driven off.

It was only, however, to direct their marauding elsewhere. In a thick bush, some fifteen feet landward from Snowy's mangrove, birds of a different sort had built a nest. They were about the same size as Snowy's parents, but instead of being white or blue as were most of the other birds he had seen, these were a metallic greenish purple. And instead of the straight beaks of the herons, their bills were longer, downcurved and blunt. They were excellent instruments for digging crabs or other denizens of the mud out of holes, but as weapons they left much to be desired.

These birds were *Glossy Ibis*. In spite of the in-effectual fighting bills, they were aggressive in defense of their territory within the colony and had driven the friendly small herons away from the nesting sites the ibis wanted. Three pairs occupied a small enclave by themselves.

Despite their hostility toward others, between them-selves the ibis displayed great affection. A little behind most of the herons, they were still incubating their eggs. The mother did most of the setting, but father relieved her twice a day so she could go out and feed. All through the incubation, whenever he returned, he would invariably find a stick or two and add it to the nest before settling down for his trick on the eggs. By the time the young were ready to leave it, the ibis nest would be twice as big as when the eggs were laid.

When the father ibis came to relieve the mother she would go directly out to feed, her hunger outweighing all else. But when she returned after two or three hours, the father would rise from his setting, and, for a quarter of an hour, with guttural *coos*, they would rub their bills and necks together and preen each other's feathers.

It was the father who was on the nest the morning the crows came. Beaten off by Snowy's mother and the other herons, the black pillagers began darting at the ibis. Gamely he tried to ward them off with his curious downcurved bill. He did get some help from the other ibis but, since they were off by themselves and the attack seemed to offer no immediate threat to the rest of the colony, they got no help from the herons.

The attacking crows realized that the blunt bills could not impale them as a heron's sharp weapon could, so they pressed on. Valiantly the ibis resisted but the crows came closer until one, more daring than the others, darted behind the defending father and seized an egg. As the beleaguered bird turned to try to stop the theft, the other crows also snatched up eggs.

With their loot in their beaks, the three robbers rose into the air, only to be assailed by a swarm of other crows. Cawing loudly they chased the egg-laden ones out of sight, trying to harass them into dropping their burden so others might try to seize it.

Soon the mother ibis returned from her feeding to find her mate off the nest and the precious eggs gone. At first both birds seemed bewildered by their loss, flying about aimlessly. But soon they were cooing and preening each other's feathers as before. It would not be long before they would have another nestful of eggs to care for.

A few days later, Snowy had another lesson in why one of his parents always stood guard. In a nearby nest were some other young egrets like himself, three of them, a day or two older than he. Their mother was standing over them, shading them from the sun with her partially opened wings. But she and the babies were getting restless. She had not had a chance to feed for some time, and all were getting ravenously hungry.

No longer did the babies doze. Angrily they pecked at their mother, demanding the food their father was supposed to bring them. But where was he? For several hours they waited and still he did not return.

What had happened? It could be any of a number of things. In a moment's carelessness, concentrating a little too intently on the water in hopes of snaring a minnow, the talons of a hawk or eagle could close on him. Standing too close to a place of concealment in a meadow, the teeth of a feral cat could sink into his neck. Wading into water a little too deep, and again a moment of relaxed wariness, an alligator's jaws might seize him.

These and countless other dangers were the constants of life. A bird would just vanish. Which of these evils had befallen him? His mate would never know.

But in this case she did know that her own hunger and that of her babies could wait no longer. Often, in cases like this, a stray single bird, usually a one-year-old who had been unable to get a mate in the competition with older birds, might show up. Then a new pair would be formed and the work of raising the youngsters would go on. Now, however, there was no unattached male in sight. And there was no more time. The mother would just have to risk it. Reluctantly she took off for the feeding grounds.

But the risk was too great. She had been gone only a few minutes when the warning came: *awrk . . awrk . . awrk!* A crow dropped from the sky. Another, seeing him go down, followed as did several others. Neighboring herons were alert, guarding their own nests but it was all over too fast for any organized defense.

Ignoring their agonizing, panicked screams, the predators seized the youngsters in their black beaks and flew off, swallowing the still struggling babies as they went.

These were not the only times Snowy felt more secure with a parent to guard him. One day he woke from a doze, wonderingly. Nothing had told him a parent was returning with food and he wasn't conscious of hearing anything. Then, at the edge of the nest, he saw a naked, featherless head. Beady eyes stared at him and a forked tongue flicked out of a threatening mouth. Back of this horror was a long, tan, sinuous body stretched out along the branch. It was a *Rat Snake* that somehow had established himself on the Key. Snowy and his brother and sister let out cries of alarm simultaneously and shrank back to the far side of the nest.

Alerted, their father, sounding the alarm and crying with anger, leaped between them and the snake. Striking at it with his bill he forced it back. The snake gave up without much struggle. He had no desire to attract one of the larger herons who would turn the tables and make a meal out of him.

Snowy was growing fast and learning fast. He would need both the strength and the knowledge. The strength was coming two ways: from the unending supplies of food brought by his parents as each made several trips a day to and from the feeding grounds, and from exercising. The learning came largely from watching his parents, his brother and sister, and other birds.

The three babies were able to stand quite steadily now and move about. While waiting, usually impatiently, to be fed, they would spend a lot of time jumping up and down, flapping their tiny stubs of wings, pecking at their parents, at twigs in the nest, or at each other. Vital muscles were being used and getting stronger.

When he was ten days old, Snowy began to feel an itching on his skin. He was not a thing of beauty like his parents. His down was pure white and almost an inch long around his head, but elsewhere it was rather sparse. His bill and legs were not the shiny black of older birds, but a sort of pale yellow. And the naked spots of skin under the down were greenish. He was rather scrawny and his head and feet were still too large for his body.

But now he was going to change. Little pinpoints of hard matter were pressing up along his flesh. By the next day it could be seen that these were sheaths and they were beginning to break open. He was fledging, getting his feathers.

Imitating his parents' preening, he kept nibbling at them, which relieved the itch and at the same time helped the growth along. And often one of his parents would lean over and help him, pecking away to remove the scaly sheaths as the feathers emerged.

He had to learn early that his life would depend on his feathers. Although he would be able to replace any that were lost, and he would get all new ones every year and some new ones twice a year, feathers nevertheless required constant care.

For hours he would watch his parents preening theirs. Next to caring for their youngsters, feeding, and the constant alert for danger, feather-care seemed to occupy them most. A parent on guard duty would nibble at the "powder downs" under his breast feathers. These were tiny feathers that crumbled into a white dust. With this the old bird would meticulously clean each feather, running it carefully through his bill. Often he would also comb his feathers with a special toothed projection nature had given all members of the heron family. This was almost literally a tiny comb on an elongated middle toe. It could smooth and clean feathers the bill could not reach and was also useful in scratching or getting rid of lice and other parasites that sometimes bother birds. With his bill, or "toe comb," Snowy's parent would take particular care to clean off any spots made dirty by contact with mud or food. Feathers had to be kept in constant readiness for flight and for warmth. When a mate returned from the feeding ground, the other spouse would always be spotless, ready for the ceremonial greeting before feeding.

There was less delay now before feedings. The growing stomachs could handle semisolids; indeed, as we have seen, Snowy's older brother had already eaten solid food. A returning parent would now regurgitate the food up into his bill and feed the babies almost at once without waiting for further digestion.

Then one day, when Snowy was two weeks old and half grown, they were all going to take a long step toward self-sufficiency. The father came in as usual with food. The three youngsters started jockeying for position, jumping up and down in their eagerness and grabbing for the parental bill. But instead of feeding them as usual, the father simply disgorged the food on the edge of the nest.

The youngsters hesitated a moment and then lunged at the food, gobbling it down as fast as they could. Pecking away between the interlaced twigs they got it all except for one piece of fish several inches long. Try as they would, fighting over it, the little ones could neither break it up with their small bills nor get it down their tiny throats.

It was an exceptionally large fish which the old bird had caught. He had had trouble swallowing it himself and most of it was still in one big piece with the rest of the meal. Finally he intervened. He plucked the piece away from his offspring and swallowed it again himself. He was not robbing his children of their food. After allowing his digestive juices to work on it a few more minutes, he simply disgorged the piece of fish a second time. Now it was soft enough so the three still hungry youngsters were able to break it up and swallow it. And hereafter they would get no more food direct from their parents' bills.

Immediately after a feeding Snowy and his brother and sister would usually lie or squat back on the side of the nest dozing, momentarily satisfied. But many times Snowy would lie awake watching his parents. Their golden yellow feet were often clasped to the edge of the nest near his head, and on the occasions when both were there, usually late afternoons, they would preen each other's feathers, working with their black bills over the white plumes on the head and upper back, the feathers the bird himself could not reach with his own bill.

This usually would be accompanied with low guttural *coos*, the cries of affection. The sun would go down and an air of peace would descend over the colony. Not that the noise ever stopped, but it seemed to go on in a some-what lower key.

The herons quieted down as they settled for the night, and even the cormorants' incessant *arrumps* were less raucous. The old pelicans, who never uttered anything but an occasional *chuck* anyway, were entirely mute and their noisy youngsters were heard from less and less. There were occasional strident interludes as a disturbed bird cried out or a night heron shrieked, but as darkness fell the world of the Key seemed less the bedlam it was by daylight.

Snowy would be less restless. He knew he could expect no more feedings until after dawn, so there was no need for the constant semialert to make sure his brother or sister did not do him out of his share of food.

The nights brought other tranquillities. Both parents were stationed at the nest, a double measure of assurance. And the crows, whose continual cawing during the day kept old and young alike in a state of some alarm, were gone. At dusk the crows made off for their own mainland nesting site—except for one pair that had built a nest right in the colony, near the hoped-for supply of food. But Snowy soon learned the crows would not bother him at night.

There were some ominous sounds in the darkness, it was true. The hooting of a large owl or the tremulous whine of a screech owl would often wake Snowy and cause him to shrink against the side of the nest, but no attacks developed from these enemies. And the Key had enough water between it and the mainland or the larger islands to ensure it against depredations by four-footed mammals. The dawn, however, brought dramatic change. This was the time of the colony's maximum activity. Polyglot cries greeted the daylight. There was a great stirring as fully half of the hundreds of various adult birds prepared to depart all at the same time.

Some of the smaller herons, usually including one of Snowy's parents, and the larger egrets would often depart in small flocks, some in one direction, others in another, depending on which feeding ground they preferred. The great blue herons, for the most part lonely hunters, would flap off individually and grandly. The ibis would form a little group of their own and head for their favorite feeding place. Cormorants and anhingas would drop from their higher nesting places directly onto the water where they would either take to the air again or swim out into the deeps for their hunting. The big, clumsy pelicans, causing a great snapping back of the branches which had born their weight during the night, would almost fall downward until, with what seemed like a desperate flapping of the big wings, they would begin to gain altitude just before striking the surface. They would then fly off to search for prey from the skies. And as all these birds were departing, the ominous black crows would return.

With each dawn Snowy felt stronger, more sure of himself. He would lie on his back, with his face and bill turned upward, watching all this coming and going. He would gaze beyond into the infinite deep blue above. Soon he began to notice that there were many things in that sky besides the friendly birds of the colony.

There were the crows, of course. He was all too familiar with them. For the most part they roosted in the tree tops in their constant hopeful waiting for an unattended nest, but some flew about over Snowy's head. And on beyond the crows, higher still, Snowy could see other, larger black figures.

These were *Vultures*. There were two kinds. One, with longer, thinner wings, soared effortlessly, floating up and down with the currents of the sky. This was the *Turkey Vulture*, a bird that might devour Snowy, but not until he was past caring.

The other was a squatter, more ominous bird with thicker, white-tipped wings. It did not soar as well as the other vulture and so flapped its wings more often. This was a *Black Vulture*, one that would not always wait until his victim was past caring, one willing to hasten the demise. A pair of these creatures, as a matter of fact, had a nest right in the colony, a dangerous menace as Snowy was going to discover.

Even farther up in the sky, above the vultures, there were still other figures, other dark birds. These had much longer, thinner wings and long, forked tails. They seemed to hang, sometimes almost motionlessly, in the air with wings outspread but unmoving, resting in the sky as other birds might rest on a perch. These were *Frigate Birds*, or *Man-o'-War Birds*. They had completed their own nesting in island colonies far to the south, and now had spread northward looking for just such a colony of lesser birds as there was on the Key.

Snowy eventually would learn that these big frigate birds were not as much of a menace to him as the crows. Occasionally, as he was going to see, one would fall on an unattended nest and snatch up a youngster or an egg, but for the most part the frigate birds were interested in fish, and bigger fish than the small herons like Snowy's parents ordinarily caught.

Often he would see one of these marauders suddenly swoop diagonally downward from his great height and disappear behind the mangroves. It wasn't until a little later, when he was able to climb up near the top of his tree, that he found out what these missions of the frigate birds were all about.

He had climbed up near a cormorant's nest, where he also discovered that all black birds were not necessarily enemies. The old cormorants, with their continual admonishing *arrumps*, seemed friendly enough, and their coal-black downy young clucked at the white stranger with cheerful curiosity. But they paid him no attention when an old cormorant came back to the nest with food. If anything, they seemed more insatiably hungry even than Snowy and his nest mates.

To get them food, the parents did not have to go as far as the herons, who sought out mud or sandy flats covered with just a little water. The old cormorants hunted in the deeper water nearby, diving from the surface and pursuing their prey under the waves. They could seize and hold a good-sized, struggling fish, and thus laden would fly back to their hungry offspring.

Snowy had not watched the cormorants for long before he knew what the downward swoop of the frigate bird meant. Not far off the Key a cormorant emerged with a good-sized fish firmly held in his hooked bill. He paddled vigorously along the surface to get up enough speed to become airborne and, as he headed for his nest, he saw the swift figure coming toward him from out of the sky.

The cormorant turned and as he did so he swallowed the fish. Even this maneuver was to be unavailing. The cormorant is a fast flier, but no match for the larger, more agile pirate that was now about to intercept him. In vain the cormorant turned and twisted. The frigate bird harried him from side to side. The cormorant refused to give up, trying every evasive movement he knew. Finally the man-o'-war became more belligerent, battering the cormorant's side and tail with his powerful bill.

This proved to be too much. Reluctantly the cormorant disgorged the freshly swallowed fish. The buccaneer ceased his harassment and neatly caught the fish before it had fallen more than a few feet. Then, tossing the fish into the air, he deftly caught it again, head first, and swallowed it himself.

Contented, the frigate bird soared upward to resume his stance in the sky. The tired cormorant, with hungry stomachs still awaiting him at the nest, could only go back into the water to fish again and hope for better luck next time.

III

ONE morning Snowy was startled to hear a sound unlike anything he had heard before. It was a sputtering roar that didn't seem to come from a living thing. As he listened it got louder, above even the din of the colony.

Others heard it too. An air of tenseness settled over the Key. Cries of alarm sounded above the roar. The bigger herons, the great blues and American egrets, raised their long necks above the trees to look out across the water. Snowy's own father and the other smaller herons and ibis stretched up, tensely alert. Cormorants and anhingas quieted their growlings and the silent pelicans stirred uneasily on their nests.

The sound grew louder, drowning out all else. And now they could see what made it. A huge thing plunging through the water directly toward the Key. Other birds that had been out getting food started returning to their mates and their nests in alarm.

Finally the thing slowed down. The sound ceased so abruptly, the sudden silence seemed ominous. The thing came to rest on a bar directly under some pelican nests and out of it stepped three Lords of the Earth. These were creatures none of the nestlings had ever seen before.

But the old birds had. And the clamor in the colony now became overpowering. Many birds started up, each crying his protest in his separate way.

The air resounded with the long *squawks* of the great blue herons and the *quoks* of the night herons as they circled above their nests. Smaller herons and egrets, like Snowy's parents, were flying about, adding their shriller cries. Cormorants and anhingas flew about growling. Even the crows, who were going to benefit from this intrusion, were cawing loudly. Only the pelicans endured their fear and anger in silence.

As the men waded ashore, the birds nearest them were seized with panic. Those on the outer edges of the colony were mostly pelicans. Ordinarily, when these ungainly birds left their nests or roosts, they took off over the open water, for inevitably they fell downward, losing altitude before they could achieve flight. But now, lest they fall into the very arms of the intruders, many were forced to take off inland. These dropped into the tangle of branches below, where their great wings became enmeshed and frantic struggles took place as they sought to untangle themselves.

The young birds, of all different kinds and ages, were

adding their noisy protests to the general bedlam. Those who were old enough, in their anxiety to put as much distance as possible between themselves and this enemy, climbed out of their nests seeking to get higher up in the trees or bushes. There they teetered unsteadily on swaying branches. Many, in their panic, vomited their half-digested food and let their excrement go, some of this often falling on the men below.

Snowy and his brother and sister, as terrified as the rest, could see their parents circling above them. But the men were still some distance away. The youngsters stayed in the nest, huddled down, panting and trembling.

Then the world of the Key seemed to come apart. There was an explosive roar, louder than anything heard before—a report that echoed through the mangroves. And as it did, a glossy ibis, who had just flown off his nest, crumpled in the air. Snowy could hear the thud of his body striking the earth.

Few of the egrets, even the older birds, had heard this noise at close range before. But it stirred something in their biological memories, something of earlier slaughtered breeding colonies and the near extermination of their kind.

Overwhelmed by surprise and panic, most of the birds were momentarily silent. Then their bedlam started up again, louder than ever. Parents who had stayed at their nests now left. Youngsters climbed farther out on unsafe perches. It was at this point that Snowy and his brother and sister struggled out of their nest and sought, on shaky legs, to climb higher, somehow to get away from this horror.

There was another shot. Another ibis fell, this time into the water. These ibis were plumper than herons, more tender and less "fishy" than cormorants and pelicans. It was a suitability for the palates of men for which they were now paying.

Suddenly, even through the echo of the shots and the noise of the panicked and infuriated birds, there was another sound. It was another roar in the distance, out in the sound. Evidently the gunmen heard this too, for they started running for their boat. Snowy could hear its roar as it made off at high speed, and then the roar of the other boat increasing as it set out in pursuit.

The Key was once again left to its inhabitants. But the havoc of the visit was only beginning.

Snowy and his sister were out on a limb several feet from their nest. A slight breeze arose and they teetered perilously. With their beaks they managed to get hold of a branch above them and, with half-formed wings outspread and using all their feeble strength, they clung. Unknown but terrifying perils lay below. No matter how the muscles ached, they dare not let go.

They managed to cling on, but their older brother was not so lucky. He was bigger and stronger than they and had ventured farther from the nest, onto a more unsteady limb.

Crying out, he sought to get hold of another branch with his beak but missed. Swaying back and forth, crying in terror, his feet clung as tenaciously as they could. But it was not enough. His young, tired muscles could not maintain the unsteady perch. Down he fell to the earth below where his feeble screams continued.

This tragedy was being repeated all over the colony. And other evils were now befalling it. Parent birds, in their terror, had left eggs and nestlings unguarded. The ever-lurking crows were taking advantage of this.

In this there were conflicts of basic impulses. All were still fearful of the men. For the parent birds the pull of responsibility and the desire to protect and care for their young was being weighed against this fear. For the maurauders it was the pull of hunger that was being weighed against the fear. In some cases the parents beat the crows to the nests, in others the crows got there first.

It was the crows who came first and stayed longest, but with so many tempting opportunities others were also on hand to take advantage of the situation.

From his high, still perilous vantage point, Snowy could look directly down into a Louisiana heron's nest with three eggs. Parents with eggs did not experience as strong a pull to return as did those with young. Both of Snowy's parents had now returned, but the blue eggs of the heron were still unguarded. Silently, over the limbs, glided the long rat snake that had so terrified Snowy a few days before. With little trouble he engulfed the three eggs, finishing the last one and slithering off just as the screaming herons returned.

Farther below him, in the middle of a cactus patch, Snowy could see the large nest of the bigger, American egret. Two babies had left it and fallen to the ground. One, too small to climb out of the nest, was still there. Suddenly there was the shadow of long slender wings. Out of the sky dropped a frigate bird and deftly snatched up the screaming youngster.

Until now the frigate birds had contented themselves with their normal pursuit, robbing old birds of their fish. But predators as well as prey have adaptability. This was too good an opportunity for a change of diet to be missed. Snowy could see other slender shadows and hear the frightened squawks of young cormorants and pelicans above him as they, too, were being seized by the big pirates of the sky.

Little by little parents were now returning. When there was anything left to save, they usually succeeded in driving the robbers off. But in many cases it was too late. Birds whose eggs and young were gone were flying about in bewilderment.

Snowy and his sister, meanwhile, at the continued chucking commands and encouragement of their parents, were painstakingly making their way back to their nest. Still panting and trembling in terror, they finally managed to make it safely. Other youngsters throughout the colony also were being coaxed back into their nests, if they could make it. So at last things were returning to normal in the trees.

But not on the ground. Here the final grim chapter of the visit of the men was being played out.

Like other birds, Snowy's parents searched through the branches for the missing member of their family, the elder son. They did not seek him on the ground. Something told them if he had fallen to earth he was beyond their help.

And on the ground he was one of many beyond saving. Some crows, chased from the nests by returning parents, were there too, after these earthbound victims. But in this new environment there was another, more formidable enemy. . . .

Almost directly below him, Snowy could see this huge black creature, twice as big as the crow and twice as frightening, with a naked, featherless head of wrinkled black skin. This was the black vulture, now seen at terrifyingly close range, the scavenger who, unlike its more peaceful cousin, the turkey vulture, did not always wait for its victims to die.

This truth was now being demonstrated. One of these vultures up in the sky, seeing the helpless fledglings frantically running for cover after the men had left, had dropped down among them. Another, seeing him break the flight pattern, had followed, then others.

One, more foresighted, was already at the feast. She had thoughtfully made her nest, a hollowed out space beneath a thick bush, right in the center of the colony. She was always there on the alert for any baby that might fall from a nest or the trees. This bird had two hungry young vultures of her own to feed, and while the motors of the departing boats were still audible, she had fallen on her victims.

Now, joined by others from the sky, they quickly chased the crows away and were busy seizing the screaming, panicked little herons, cormorants, and pelicans as, on their feeble legs, they vainly sought shelter under bushes or cacti.

The vultures lacked talons that could tear the flesh of adult birds, but the tender babies were a different matter. It didn't last long. Soon the cries of the babies ended and only the crunching of the vultures tearing at them could be heard.

Finally this, too, quieted down and only the normal noises of the colony remained, with one exception. A pelican, still entangled in a maze of branches and mangrove roots, was struggling to get free. The sounds of his thrashings, becoming weaker and weaker, went on through the night until his body hung motionless in its trap.

Early next morning the birds could hear another boat approaching the Key. Again the alarms were sounded, the protests voiced. This time two different men waded ashore. They shook their heads silently as they examined the remains of dead birds. Carefully they retrieved the dead pelican from the mangrove branches and the ibis, which had fallen on the earth and which the gunners had abandoned. These birds, at least, would live on in museum collections.

The new visitors moved about slowly and quietly and the birds began calming down a little. But then the new intruders themselves started after the young birds. Cries of protest increased.

One of the men came climbing up the tree in which Snowy's nest was located. There were many nests in this tree, those of other small egrets, of little blue and Louisiana herons. Panic seized the inhabitants of all of them.

Tiny babies shrank, squawking feebly, to the far sides of their nests. Older ones, panting and trembling and crying out more loudly, climbed out of their nests and sought the questionable safety of the higher limbs. Some tumbled to the ground.

The parents, including Snowy's, were torn between fury and fear, between the urge to try to save their young and the urge to protect themselves. The result was a compromise between the two drives. Screaming loudly, they flew around the head of the intruder, some coming within only a few feet, hoping this way he might be frightened off. But none dared try to drive him away with actual physical attack.

The climber paid no attention to them at all. He continued on up the tree, closer to the nestlings and the fleeing fledglings. Snowy and his sister had scrambled out of their nest again. She, with remarkable agility, made her way toward the upper branches. But Snowy, just as he got over the rim of the nest, found his oversized foot trapped in a crotch between a limb and the nest. Frantically he struggled to work it free. The harder he pulled, the more firmly did his little leg remain in its trap. Desperately he flapped his wings, crying out in panic.

At last he felt the twigs of the nest loosening. His leg pulled free. But just at that moment he felt himself imprisoned. The big hand of the intruder closed around him. Squawking more loudly than ever, Snowy jabbed viciously with his sharp bill at the soft flesh of the hand. The firm, although gentle, grip did not relax. Snowy was carried down onto the ground.

By now his terror and exhaustion were so complete, he stopped resisting altogether. He lay panting, his eyes wide. But instead of being crushed to death, he was held gently. His captor slipped something around Snowy's leg and clamped it on.

He then carried the little bird back up in the tree and placed him carefully back in the nest. Snowy now had an adornment around his leg he would carry the rest of his life. It was a metal band with the legend:

Advise Fish & Wildlife Service
Write Washington D. C. U. S. A.
869–62792

For several hours the two men stayed on the Key capturing and banding all the young birds they could conveniently get their hands on. They even found the vulture's nesting place, although they had to crawl through a thicket to get to it, and put bands on two baby vultures.

The parent birds were still flying about, crying their protests, but they were getting calmer all the time. The youngsters who fell to earth or into the water this time were carefully returned to their nests by the men.

The crows and frigate birds and vultures dared not commit their depredations while the men were on the Key. And by the time they were ready to leave, the parent birds were mostly reassured enough to get back to their nests before their enemies arrived.

There were some casualties. A few crows did manage to slip in ahead of parents, and a few young tumbled down which the men overlooked, but nothing like the havoc of the day before.

By the next day it all seemed to have been forgotten. The inexorable business of setting, brooding, preening, teaching, eating, and being eaten resumed. Those who had lost eggs and those who had lost young, if the young had not been too old, simply reverted to the courting and lovemaking of their earlier mating and started all over again.

IV

By the time Snowy was three weeks old, he spent most of the daylight hours outside the nest. He and his sister climbed about the tree and perched on nearby branches, sunbathing, preening their own and each other's feathers.

They never ventured far. For one thing the tree was crowded with nests and they had to be careful not to encroach upon another's domain. Also, they had their own rights to look after.

One day, as they were dozing on a limb a few feet away, a neighboring young egret several days older than they, climbed into their empty nest. Snowy saw him first. With a valiant, almost adult *awrk . . awrk!*, Snowy, flapping his wings, raced along the limb and began jabbing his beak at the much larger intruder. The trespasser scrambled out and retreated without much fuss. Territorial rights must be understood early in life.

When they were out of the nest, Snowy and his sister were never far apart. Each wanted to be first when a parent returned with food. And what a rush on these occasions! Snowy always hoped his father or mother would bring the food out onto the limb where they were, for the run back to the nest, aided by the flapping of his little wings, was tiring. And run he must, or his sister would get everything.

As a matter of fact, this exercise was building up muscles that would be necessary for Snowy's survival, muscles that would enable him to run and fly swiftly. And the parents aided this development in other ways. Often they seemed purposely to drop the food in among the twigs of the nest where it would be hard to extricate. Sometimes the young muscles of Snowy's neck would ache from the exertion of trying to get it out before his sister did. He was developing speed, force, and accuracy with his sharp bill.

As the days passed Snowy's feathers sprouted out at a remarkable rate. He spent hours preening them, coaxing the growth along, keeping them clean and dry, ready for instant flight. And how he wanted to fly! When he was not eating or preening or sunning himself, he loved to do a little dance. Flapping his wings vigorously with a jump, he would lift himself up into the air. Gradually he got braver and could jump up a foot or two this way. But he was always careful to see that he could land back safely on his limb. He was all too familiar with the perils that lay below.

Then one day, when Snowy was about five weeks old, a strange thing happened. He and his sister, hungry as usual, were on a branch above the nest when they heard their father returning from the feeding grounds. Crying eagerly, they dropped onto the lower limb, flapped, and ran to the nest. But this time their parent landed on another branch, several feet away.

The youngsters cried out angrily, demanding that he bring the food as usual. Instead he stood calmly on the limb out of their reach. They could see that he held in his bill a plump minnow, food that they loved. Yet between them and the meal yawned a chasm six feet wide with tangled branches immediately below and all the terrors of the ground below that.

Screaming now in their anger and frustration, Snowy and his sister teetered on their perch. Hunger and fear, as it would much of their lives, competed within them.

It was the sister, still a little the larger, who leaped first. Snowy could not stand this. With all his strength he threw himself into the air, flapping his wings desperately. He saw his sister land on the limb next to his father. He felt himself moving forward but he was losing altitude fast. The limb was just too far away. Missing it by inches, Snowy plunged into the abyss below.

Fortunately his wings caught on some of the lower branches and his feet managed to secure a hold. As he lay there, frightened and panting, he looked up to see his sister swallowing the minnow. Neither his sister nor his father seemed to pay any attention to him. Survival, he was learning, was going to be a lonely business.

Carefully, with beak and neck, wings and feet, he worked his way through the swaying small branches toward the center of the tree. At last he came to a larger limb leading upward. Climbing along, he was able, finally, to get back to the nest. Tired and hungry, but safe.

By then it was evening and no more food would be coming in until morning. Snowy slept but, ravenous, he was out on the limb by the nest at dawn in time to see his father leave. His mother, as she often did, caressed his feathers, but Snowy had no thought but for the return of the other parent.

His hunger was now all demanding, conquering other sensations. When his father lit again on the branch across from him, Snowy leaped without hesitation.

This time he used his wings more effectively. His feet struck the branch but he teetered and almost fell. He grasped his father's bill in his own and steadied himself. Eagerly he took the minnow and swallowed it.

Daily thereafter it became less difficult. Between feedings now, Snowy and his sister would fly up a few feet and circle a little before coming back to their perch.

And then one morning they awoke to find both parents standing by the nest. The young birds were puzzled. Who was getting their food? Angrily, they cried out. Their mother launched herself, but instead of heading for the feeding grounds she circled about and came back. When she did this a second time, Snowy and his sister plunged out too and followed.

It was a dizzy business. Now they were out farther from their nest than ever before. Nervous, Snowy started to turn back. He almost bumped into his father, who had joined the little procession and was flying right behind him.

The youngsters flew on, following their mother. Over the last outer row of red mangroves they went. There was nothing below now but sand and mud and water. Then their mother turned down, landing gently in about an inch of water. Down came the young birds too, landing heavily with splashes, glad to rest their aching wing muscles. Their father landed right behind them with scarcely a sound.

Snowy looked about. There were other family groups nearby. In addition to other small egrets, there were families of Louisiana herons, the delicate little blue herons with their strangely contrasting all-white youngsters, and a gray and black and white night heron with his young, a dingy mottled brown.

This was a feeding ground adjacent to the Key, reserved for the oncoming generation. Food was not as plentiful here as in the more extensive feeding grounds farther out, but there was enough. And during the setting and feeding of young in the nests, most old birds avoided this area. There had to be a nearby training ground for the young.

Snowy watched his father. The old bird stood frozen, watching the water. Snowy gazed downward too. A little school of tiny minnows came by. With a quick swish, so fast Snowy could scarcely see it, his father grasped one of the little fish and lifted it, struggling, from the water. The other minnows circled about in terror. Snowy stabbed at them and missed. He would have to start with easier prey.

His father started walking slowly, putting a yellow foot out in front of him and stirring the sand ahead. A tiny crab ran out. His father made no move this time and Snowy struck.

He felt the little crustacean struggling against his bill. He grasped it firmly and with a sense of elation raised it out of the water. His triumph was premature. When he relaxed his bill slightly to swallow the morsel, the crab struggled free and scampered off. Snowy would have to start with even more sedentary prey.

At last his father's foot uncovered some insect larvae and tiny worms that couldn't get away. Greedily Snowy gulped them up. A little later, when a shrimp came by, Snowy managed to seize it. This time he carried the creature to dry land where he could drop it and quickly grab its head before it could hop away. With the struggling shrimp thus positioned, Snowy could swallow it.

This was the most exciting day of Snowy's young life. Eagerly he went about his hunting. Darkness threatened all too soon. The parent birds took to the air and reluctantly Snowy and his sister followed. He found he could fly more easily now, and he was hardly tired at all when he arrived back at the nest where they would spend the night.

At dawn Snowy could scarcely wait to get out on the flats. Not only did his hunger drive him but also the sense of excitement and power that came from searching out and overcoming an elusive and resisting prey.

But never would he be allowed to forget that at any moment he himself might become the prey, might give that sense of excitement and satisfaction to someone else. As the family was about to depart they heard a cry. *Raahnk . . raahnk . . raahnk!* It came from a nearby nest, the alarm cry of the larger American egret.

Snowy, his sister, and his parents froze. They stood motionless under the leaves of the mangrove, but ready for instant flight if it should be necessary. A sinister shadow passed over them, a hawk. But then the older birds relaxed and made ready to depart. Snowy looked up and saw the all-white undersides and black-lined head. This, then, was not an enemy to be feared.

It was a hawk as a matter of fact, but a hawk called an *Osprey*, or fish hawk, one who confined himself to hunting fish and left birds alone. Snowy was beginning to distinguish between the creatures that would harm him and those that wouldn't, even between different hawks. It was an important part of his education, for, if he wasted too much effort trying to elude the harmless, he would have that much less strength and cunning to combat his real enemies.

During the next few days Snowy learned a great deal about the business that was going to occupy most of his strength and cunning from now on—securing food. It wasn't easy. When they had made their first flight from the nest to the nearby feeding grounds, Snowy and his sister were actually larger, or at least heavier, than their parents.

The old birds had lost weight steadily as they gave up food to the growing young. The youngsters, on the other hand, had put on more than their share of fat. Now this was going to change. Dependent on what they could obtain for themselves, even with the constant help and guidance of their parents, the inexperienced young ones began slimming down. The parents, on the contrary, now able to absorb all the food they could obtain, steadily gained back their lost weight.

His parents and others like them, Snowy noticed, used many devices to catch their prey. Sometimes they stood stone-still, eyes fixed on the water below, waiting for some creature to come into view. At other times, they stirred the bottom with a yellow foot, hoping something hiding in the mud or sand would emerge. At other times they ran energetically about in active pursuit of some elusive prey.

In all these methods Snowy became constantly more adept. And he was not beyond trying new methods of his own. Once, flying back to the nest, he caught and swallowed a butterfly in midair. The general rule was: anything that moves may be eaten.

The other members of the colony, now out on these flats in increasing numbers, had their own methods of feeding, all slightly different. Some, like the Louisiana herons, ran about in pursuit of prey much more often than did the egrets. On the other hand, some, like the great blue herons, almost always stood alone and motionless, like statues on the horizon, waiting for anything that would come within range of their deadly bill. The ibis liked to feed together, grubbing into the mud with their curved bills.

Parents sometimes admonished their young for failure to abide by the rules. Snowy saw a black-crowned night heron and his youngster standing together, motionless, waiting for prey. After a while the young one grew impatient and started slowly to move. With an angry cry the old night heron struck him a vigorous blow on the back with a formidable thick bill. The young bird yelped and flew off a few feet. But thereafter, whenever his parent wanted to employ the motionless strategy in his feeding, the youngster remained still.

As the days progressed Snowy noticed that they were a little later each morning in leaving the nest. Impatient, he and his sister would prod their parents, urging that they go out to look for food. But the old birds would not leave until they were ready. Snowy would learn about tides. There was no use looking for food in some places when the water was too high.

Finally one morning they left earlier than usual. When they arrived over the accustomed feeding place the water looked quite deep but Snowy started to descend. He heard a preemptory squawk from his father behind him and noticed that his mother had not led the way downward. Instead she flew on, out over the open water.

On and on they flew. The only thing Snowy could see ahead was a vague row of mangroves that marked the beginning of the mainland. This seemed an impossible distance away but obviously that was where they were headed. It was by far the longest flight for Snowy and his wing muscles ached. Finally they were over the mangroves and beyond them Snowy could see a wide, open lagoon. Here the tide was low and there were broad, exposed flats of mud and sand.

Birds were everywhere. Many were kinds Snowy had not seen before. Most striking was a large flock, just taking off from the flats, with shining pink wings and backs blazing in the sunlight. These were *Roseate Spoonbills*, who had already nested down south and returned. Now, finished with their night of feeding, they were headed for their roosting place.

Feeding in the shallows below him were many birds almost as white as Snowy but with long red downcurved bills and reddish legs. They looked just like his ibis friends of the colony in different dress and were, in fact, *White Ibis*. They were nesting in another colony nearby.

The sky was also full of birds. Many were noisy creatures, white with darkish wings and shining black heads, who circled about continually crying out. These were the scavengers of the flats and beaches, *Laughing Gulls*, who had their own nesting colony on a sandy island in the gulf. Also circling about, more purposefully, were some smaller, more graceful birds with longer wings and forked tails. Every now and then one of these would plummet head first into the water and usually come up with a minnow struggling in his bill. These were *Least Terns* who had their own small nesting colony on a nearby sandy beach. These gulls and terns would soon be joined by other, different ones, cousins from the north.

As he got closer, Snowy could see many smaller birds of different kinds scampering over the flats. These were *Shorebirds*, some were *Wilson's* and *Snowy Plovers*, who were nesting on the beach along with the terns, and some were other plovers and *Sandpipers*, the more widely traveled ones, early arrivals back from their far north breeding grounds.

In deeper water at the edge of the mangroves, Snowy saw a fat, squat brownish bird swimming along with six fluffy little ones following, a *Mottled Duck* who would later be joined by many different cousins from the north.

Snowy, for the first time, was on one of the general feeding grounds, and his life was about to undergo a radical change.

He noticed that he and his sister were now left almost entirely to their own devices in the search for prey. In fact, once or twice when he got too close to his father, the old bird gruffly drove him away. Snowy noticed also that his parents had now lost the long, gleaming, fluffy plumes that he had seen all the time he was growing up. And with the vanishing of these feathers, affection seemed to be disappearing too. More and more the parents were getting irritable toward their offspring and sometimes toward each other.

For a few days the family stayed together, flying to this feeding ground each morning and returning to roost at the nest at night. Then one morning, instead of leaving the Key, the parents led the young birds off the nest on a circular flight, up and up. Higher and higher they rose until Snowy could see for miles around. It was a sight that would be engraved in his memory.

The mainland looked closer now, and in the other direction he could see the chain of large islands that enclosed the inland waters. At their outer edge he saw the white sand beaches, the surf, and, beyond, the open sea.

Automatically his mind registered many bayous and lagoons and, beyond the mainland mangroves, meadows and fresh-water swamps, all places where food might be obtained. He also noticed other mangrove islands and clumps of mangroves and other trees, places where a safe roost might be found.

Above all, forever implanted in his mind, was the location of his native Key and its relation to all this vast surrounding area. It was his lesson in geography. He would never forget it.

Suddenly, without warning, the parent birds dropped down, back to the Key. Snowy and his sister started to follow. But they were hungry. So, instead, they flew off without their parents for the first time and made their way to the now familiar feeding place.

Keeping a respectful distance from other birds, they fed together and that evening flew unerringly back to the Key and their nest. The parents were already there and the four slept as usual. But when the young birds awoke the next morning, their parents were gone.

Snowy and his sister flew again to the flats. There was

no sign of their parents there. The family ties, so close during the preceding weeks, had ended. The parents, in fact, had departed separately. The pair bond, no longer essential, was dissolved. When the time came, they would find new mates for the next season. Snowy's sister soon flew off to another part of the feeding grounds and then left to seek a new area. He did not follow.

Snowy was now on his own.

V

It was late afternoon by now and Snowy knew he had to have a roosting place for the night. There was only one place he had ever spent a night so he flew back to the Key. He expected to sleep in his nest as always, but that was not to be. For the nest, at least what was left of it, was occupied by someone else, someone who had no intention of letting him share it.

When Snowy arrived at his home mangrove, he saw standing by his nest a white bird about the same size as himself, but stockier and with shorter legs, neck, and bill. And instead of white plumes, its head and neck were covered with short brownish feathers. It was a *Cattle Egret,* recent immigrant to the New World from Africa. Late nesters, these birds were getting ready to raise their young just as the native herons were finishing.

At the moment Snowy arrived, the cattle egret was engaged in an altercation with a Louisiana and a little blue heron, both of whom were attempting to steal sticks from Snowy's already partially dismantled old nest. The cattle egret, however, was holding them at bay.

The raiders were bigger and had much longer, sharper bills. But the cattle egret had an overriding advantage. He was defending. When Snowy's family abandoned their territory, the newcomer had laid claim to it. Somehow, a bird defending his own territory was known by the others to have right on his side. Or, since his motive was strongest, it was known that eventually he would win out anyway and losing causes never serve any purpose. Thus Snowy, when it was *his* nest, had been able to drive away other young birds who tried to encroach even when they were bigger than he. Here the cattle egret was holding off the invasion of better-armed antagonists because now it was *his* nest.

Soon the would-be twig snatchers left. Snowy made only a halfhearted attempt to reclaim his old home. A defiant gesture on the part of the occupier was sufficient to send him on his way.

But where to sleep? He flew about, landing on several likely looking branches, but always there turned out to be someone's nest nearby. Angry cries warned him that he was trespassing. Finally he found a sheltered perch near the center of the colony that was far enough away from the surrounding nests so the occupants suffered him to remain.

By now Snowy was very tired. He had no trouble

relaxing on his perch. Like most birds, as soon as he bent his legs in the roosting position, the tendons automatically tightened and his feet held firmly to the branch without effort on his part. He was relaxed, but far from content.

Snowy was one of the most gregarious of birds. Nesting, traveling, roosting, and, although at times he would seek food alone, even in most of his feeding, he would be content only in company with others of his kind. He finally fell asleep, but he knew that tomorrow he would have to find a roosting flock.

As always, Snowy awoke hungry. He was still too unsure of himself to venture any farther from routine than he had to, so he flew back to the only general feeding ground he knew. There seemed to be even more birds of more different kinds there than there had been before. On one mud flat, covered by only a few inches of water, Snowy saw a group of about a dozen small herons, mostly little egrets like himself. Down he came and landed near the center of them. It was not the proper approach.

One old male egret, who seemed to stand taller, more erect than the rest, half opened his wings, raised his head and neck feathers and, with a cry of warning, advanced toward the newcomer. The other birds all stopped to watch. Snowy had no intention of getting into a quarrel or of challenging this dominant bird. He retreated hastily, backing away and keeping an eye on the antagonist lest he be surprised by a sudden lunge.

When Snowy had reached the extreme edge of the group, the old bird closed his wings and turned back. The other birds resumed their feeding. He could remain, provided he recognized his place at the very bottom of the peck order.

Feeling at least partly accepted, Snowy set about trying to satisfy his hunger. This was seldom easy. Each tide brought in a bountiful supply of small animals and left them on these flats, but each of them was equipped with his own special devices to escape Snowy's eyes or bill. Getting a full stomach required effort, cunning, and luck.

Snowy noticed that most of the others in the group— about half were old birds and about half youngsters like himself—were using the "stand and wait" technique. They were in a good place for minnows, and these active little swimmers were usually caught with patience, simply waiting until they came within reach rather than seeking them out.

Alarmed by motion, the fish would be apt to scoot into deeper water. Thus the smaller herons would be deprived of a meal, but it might not do the fish any good. For, posted farther out, in the deeper water, were the longer-legged waders, great blue herons and the bigger egrets, awaiting just such a movement. And those minnows who avoided this hungry second line faced, in the still deeper water, cormorants diving from the surface and pelicans and terns diving from the sky. And of course still farther out were the bigger fish ready to swallow them. Altogether, the minnow's chance of survival was not high.

None of this, of course, bothered Snowy, intent only on securing one for his own survival. Like the other birds he stood without the slightest movement, staring intently into the water, neck and bill back ready to strike. Finally he was rewarded by the sight of a school of minnows approaching. He waited until they were directly in front, in easy reach, and struck. But, quick as he was, the fish were quicker. He missed and they vanished into the deep. Snowy still had much to learn.

Little fish were the quickest, most elusive, of the prey he sought. After this disappointment, commanded by his demanding stomach, he decided to try for something else. He adopted another method, the "slow wade" technique. He was sure there was better hunting where most of the birds were, but he had no desire to raise the hackles of the older birds. So he walked away from them, wading very slowly. Every now and then he would stretch his yellow right foot out in front of him and vibrate it just above the surface of the mud.

He uncovered some insect larvae which he ate and when his stirring foot sent a crab scurrying from cover Snowy managed to pick him up and swallow him all in one motion. Sometimes luck played for him. Once a careless water beetle swam right under his deadly bill and made an immediate morsel for the hungry bird.

Behind him Snowy could see some of the other birds, mostly the Louisiana herons, employing a third hunting technique, "disturb and pursue." They were running actively about, sometimes with wings outspread, and grabbing at whatever was stirred up by their activity. Snowy wasn't ready to try this yet, but he would later on.

The water was getting deeper all the time, and soon the tide had covered the flat enough so that hunting was difficult and there was the danger that an alligator or some other large beast might come along and hunt the hunters. The old egret who had put Snowy in his place gave a cry and took to the air. The others followed. They flew to a bank on the edge of the lagoon where they landed to rest, preen their feathers, and sunbathe.

Snowy's hunger was far from satisfied but he wasn't

ready yet to seek food on his own. Besides, his feathers were damp and had some soiled spots from insect larvae he had dropped while swallowing. Like the others he broke his "powder downs" and with the dry, crumbly dust carefully cleaned each feather.

As he often did, he pecked at the metal band around his leg, trying to get it off. It didn't really bother him, and most of the time he wasn't even conscious of its being there. But he knew it was not properly a part of him.

With this all done he yawned, stretched himself, and, opening his wings halfway and letting them droop down, dozed as he bathed in the now powerful rays of the sun.

Snowy, it turned out, was not the only one who was still hungry. The water in the lagoon remained quite high when the old bird again led the little group into the air. So, instead of seeking another exposed mud flat, he headed inland. After flying a mile or so over mangroves and waterways, they came to an open field of short grass. In its center was a small fresh-water pond, and here the old bird brought his followers down.

This was a new type of hunting for Snowy. There were choice morsels along the edge of the pond all right, but the grass, which grew clear into the water, made them hard to detect and gave them splendid opportunities to hide or flee unseen.

Snowy carefully watched the older birds in the flock and saw that most were adopting the "stand and wait" tactics. He did the same, and before long he saw a little frog coming to the surface. Snowy remained motionless while the amphibian took a couple of strokes toward shore. Then he struck, this time with speed and accuracy. The little animal was struggling in his bill and Snowy dared not loosen his grip in order to swallow it.

He looked about and saw a nearby bird holding a wiggling minnow and beating it against the surface of the water. Snowy tried the same maneuver. He found that after slapping his victim against the water a few times the struggling ceased. The frog was then swallowed with ease. There were many tricks Snowy still had to pick up but he was making progress.

Soon the lengthening shadows signaled time to head for the roost. Snowy heard a cry from the old bird who had led them to the pond. The flock took flight once more. Back across the lagoon they flew and out over the open sound. To his right Snowy could see the Key where he had started life but the flock did not turn in that direction. Instead they flew clear across the sound to the large outer island. Ahead Snowy could see the white beaches and the open gulf. About a mile before they got that far, however, the flock started down. Below was a wide marsh with cattails, grass, and other vegetation. Near the center was a cluster of mangroves several hundred feet in diameter rising some fifteen feet above the marsh. This was where they landed.

Quite a few birds were already there. Snowy could recognize many familiar kinds. Some of the larger egrets had already settled down for the night. Some anhingas had also found perches, and a great blue heron was roosting high up near the center.

By far the most numerous, however, were the white ibis. They came sweeping in, flock after flock, their black wing tips and long reddish legs and bills contrasting with their white bodies and, unlike the herons who folded their long necks back in flight, with neck and beak extended. These ibis usually landed first in the nearby water to drink and bathe before going up into the trees.

Snowy's little group landed near the tree tops and worked its way down to lower branches. There were other small egrets and herons already there and others were arriving all the time. There were continual cries of protest and a great deal of bickering and pecking as the birds established themselves. Usually the dominant ones took the roosts they liked and others scrambled for what was left.

Snowy's first night in his new roosting place away from the Key passed uneventfully. He finally established a place he could call his own and, tired as he was, carefully preened his feathers before falling off to sleep, his long yellow feet firmly gripped around a branch.

Several times he was awakened. Often there were cries of protest from some bird jostled by a too close neighbor, and night herons came and went with their *quok . . quok . . quoks*. There were unfamiliar sounds too. The hooting of owls was much closer and there were snarling, strident cries from raccoons some distance away. Occasionally there were splashes of large beasts resounding in the water below.

But Snowy felt a measure of security and contentment in among the mangrove branches. For now there were birds of his own and closely related kinds above, below, and on all sides of him.

In the morning, hungry as always, Snowy took off with his adopted flock and returned to the mud flats across the sound. Thus it went without particular incident for several days: on the flats at low tide, a rest when the water got higher, and then other feeding grounds before re-turning to the roost for the night.

Some of the older birds left the flock to join others or go off on their own and some new young birds appeared. Snowy was no longer at the bottom of the order and now chased other birds from his feeding territory about as often as he was admonished to keep his distance by the more established members of the group.

Through it all he was constantly gaining proficiency in the securing of prey. He had to, for the struggle was getting tougher. Multitudes of hungry competitors were arriving daily from the north.

Snowy already had noticed the active little brownish-gray shorebirds that scampered back and forth along the edges of the water. They had now been joined by count-less cousins from the north. Many of the newcomers had traveled all the way from the Arctic Circle; some would stay only a little while and go on farther south, others would remain all winter.

They were of many different kinds: *Dunlins, Sander-lings* and other little sandpipers, the plumper plovers of assorted sizes, the *Dowitchers* plunging their long bills energetically in and out of the mud, spotted sandpipers with their peculiar teetering motion.

These birds offered little competition to Snowy. They fed on tiny morsels eked out of the mud or sand or, when they sought other prey, they did so only in the shallowest water, not venturing out where the herons liked to hunt. In fact, there was an occasion when Snowy and his flock had reason to be grateful to one of these shorebirds.

It happened one day when the egrets were feeding along the edge of a fresh-water pond. There was high grass growing right up to the edge of the pool and grass in the water.

Snowy had just mastered a new trick. He discovered that if he stirred with his foot near the surface instead of down or near the bottom as he did in more open water, he could get better results. By holding his foot out and keeping it high enough to wave just the top of the grass, he found he could often scare out some elusive animal-cule and still leave the water clear enough so he could see to strike.

The game took great concentration and Snowy was engrossed, too engrossed as it turned out. Nearby was a bird about half Snowy's size. He was streaked gray and white with a long bill even more slender than Snowy's and with long, bright yellow legs. He was, in fact, a *Yellowlegs*, a shorebird cousin of the sandpipers and plovers. He was also called a "tattler," a nickname he was about to justify.

The yellowlegs, or tattler, was as usual running back and forth in active pursuit of tiny prey. Snowy could just see the movement out of the side of his eye. Suddenly the bird stopped. He took to the air with a loud, whistling cry. *Wheeet . . wheet . . wheet!*

It was a clear warning of danger. Snowy flew up too and gave his warning. *Awrk . . awrk . . awrk.* The other egrets were doing the same. Once in the air they saw it. Only a few feet from where Snowy had been feeding was a lithe and sinister monster, hidden in the long grass through which it had stolen so silently. It was a feral house cat, the unattended pet of some Lord of the Earth or a descendant thereof. An unnatural foe, particularly difficult to combat. But this time, thanks to the timely warning of the shorebird, the cat had been done out of its prey.

And Snowy had learned more lessons in the business

of survival. It is not wise to stand too close to cover from which one might be ambushed. And, while it is necessary to concentrate to secure food, if one concentrates too raptly, he is apt to become food himself.

If the shorebirds did not offer Snowy direct competition, there were many other new arrivals from the north who did. Mostly they consisted of a great influx of his own kind and of all the other herons. Flock after flock of his kith and kin were crowding his favorite flats and ponds and marshes, hungrily seeking the food on which Snowy depended.

It was mostly the young herons who arrived from the north first. Like Snowy's, their parents had put them out on their own, but unlike Snowy, these northerners had been unable to find feeding places at home not already overcrowded by older birds. Marshes and ponds and swamps that once supported thousands had disappeared. Rivers and lakes that once teemed with life were now polluted and devoid of food.

From what was left of the shrinking wetlands the younger and less dominant older birds had been driven away. They had been driven south before their time and would be driven farther south as the shortening days and falling temperatures brought many of their parents along behind them.

Besides the many members of the big heron family, there were other newcomers too. Out in the deeper water Snowy noticed some birds almost as tall as the biggest bird he knew, the great blue heron. These were stockier creatures, white with black wing tips and with thick, heavy bills and bald, featherless heads like the vultures Snowy remembered with horror. But these birds were friendly enough, only offering additional competition in the search for food. They were *Wood Ibis*, or storks, who had completed their nesting in the inland cypress swamps and had come to forage in more open waters.

Overhead the laughing gulls had been joined now by great numbers of larger, whiter gulls who circled about crying constantly, ever ready to swoop down and snatch a morsel right out of one's bill if one were careless. These were *Ring-Billed Gulls*. In among them were a few even larger, mottled brownish birds, young *Herring Gulls* forced south because their parents had occupied all the strategic points at home.

There remained few of the little least terns that Snowy had seen earlier. They had finished their nesting and were leaving for points farther south. They were, however, being replaced by different kinds of larger terns arriving from the north. These would often dive into the water just in front of Snowy, snatching up a minnow that he might have caught.

A lot of prey was also lost to a relative of the terns who had been there all summer. It was a bird as big as the gulls, with long wings, black on top and white underneath, and with one of the oddest bills Snowy had ever seen. It was bright red with a black tip and with the lower mandible protruding out way beyond the upper. These were *Black Skimmers*. Utterly ignoring Snowy, they would fly just over the water, that long lower mandible cutting a trough and sucking up minnows and other food almost in reach of Snowy's bill.

In addition to the overcrowded feeding grounds, Snowy's roost was getting much too populated. And that was going to lead to tragedy.

Snowy had been going back to the roost with his flock as the shadows lengthened each afternoon. And each time there was more and more bickering over perching places before the birds could settle for the night. Many of the northerners were crowding into the mangrove clump and, since some were the larger egrets and great blue herons and the often pugnacious Louisiana herons, Snowy and his fellows were being forced into less desirable roosts.

In Snowy's case, the larger and more forceful birds were taking places nearer the top of the trees, and he was thus getting onto lower and lower branches each night. There were still birds less dominant than he, however, and these were driven down even closer to the water.

So it came about that Snowy was awakened one night by terrifying sounds. A loud splash in the water, then a snapping crack like a tree falling. A little egret, roosting just below Snowy, screamed in mortal terror. She was being pulled down into the water. Monstrous jaws had cracked shut on her legs.

An alligator, always awaiting a bird that perched too low, had leaped up and seized her. The whole roosting colony was now awake. Terrified birds, crying their warnings in all their different ways, were forcing their way through the branches and getting into the air to fly from this danger. But this, too, would lead to tragedy.

Snowy heard another agonized cry. It was from one of the Louisiana herons who had taken his old perch and thus was in the air above him. On noiseless wings an owl had struck. Like the alligator below he waited above, hoping for just such a chance.

Snowy and most of the other birds now went back into the protective branches of the trees. They were nervous and trembling, but after a while they got re-settled and went back to sleep. Their world gave them little time for remorse, and even less for trying to figure out the meaning of things. Anyway, they would never have looked on either the owl or the alligator as a bene-factor, but in an important way the big reptile was.

The alligators who lived in these marshes, as did alligators everywhere, preyed mostly on fish. But, as we have seen, they were not inclined to pass up other food if it were offered. But alligators cannot climb trees. And their presence saved Snowy and his fellows from attacks by prowling predators that could climb trees and thus could be a greater menace.

As long as the alligators were there, no raccoon or other tree-climbing mammal dared try to cross the water to disturb the roosting birds.

VI

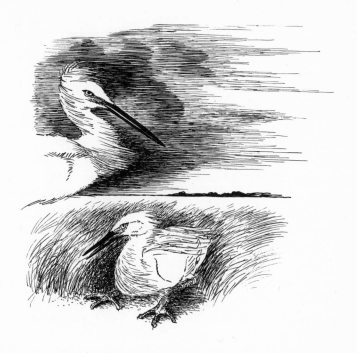

SNOWY's life was becoming increasingly difficult. Days passed without further incident, but feeding and roosting places were getting more crowded all the time. Now a greater proportion of the new arrivals were older birds. The lot of youngsters like Snowy was becoming precarious. And perhaps most disturbing of all, his flock was breaking up. Most of the other young birds had left, squeezed out and forced to look elsewhere for less crowded habitats. The time came when inner urgings bade Snowy, too, to go elsewhere.

To travel, as to do most things, he needed company.

But there were many others facing the same problem, so it was not long before, one morning, he saw half a dozen birds like himself, two older ones and four youngsters, heading away from the roost in a new direction. Snowy joined them.

They were flying south along the coast. They flew over the white beaches and surf and then over miles of mangrove jungles until they turned inland and swept on over seas of grass interspersed with hummocks of cabbage palms.

Below, Snowy could see birds of all kinds feeding in the grassy marshes, the open ponds, and along canals. But the old bird leading the flock did not stop until they reached the end of the grassy plain. Finally he brought them down on a mud flat facing several miles of open water studded with mangrove islands.

They were looking out over Florida Bay toward the Keys. Here there were many birds of many kinds and also lots of room, a great expanse of shallows, mud and sand flats, and oyster bars. They landed among a group of sandpipers who went right on feeding, undisturbed.

Snowy's group, by now voraciously hungry, waded out beyond the little shorebirds and started hunting. The mud seemed full of worms, insects, insect larvae, and other sustaining fare as well as many minnows, crabs, shrimps, and tiny crawfish. After an hour or so of feeding, the little flock was content to rest on the dry beach and preen their feathers.

By now day was drawing to a close and a roosting place must be found. Soon the flock leader took to the air, the others following. They circled over several of the small mangrove islands until they found one occupied by only a few other birds. There they settled down for the night with only minor cries of protest from the occupants. One or two other small flocks of herons came in later, but there was room for all.

As the days went by in this new southern retreat, Snowy continued to learn more about feeding. And he met some new birds. He discovered that, in the large expanses of shallow water, the "disturb and pursue" technique often served best. He would move about, working his feet up and down in the muddy sand until a good many little creatures had been flushed out and were scurrying about, bewildered. Then Snowy would run actively around, grabbing as many as he could before they found new hiding places.

He had previously seen Louisiana herons in hot pursuit of prey this way, but now he was going to meet the most active herons of them all. These were a little larger than Snowy, most a buffish blue with maroon plumes along the neck and head, but a few as pure white as Snowy himself. They were *Reddish Egrets* in the red- and white-color phases.

When Snowy first saw one, he thought the bird was in trouble. He was running about in circles, reeling from side to side with both wings outspread. But there was method in this mad rambling. Little marine animals, disturbed by the commotion, would scurry into the shadows under the wings. It was usually their last hiding place.

As a contrast Snowy soon made a better acquaintance with the largest and least active of his heron cousins, the great blue and great white herons. Snowy watched one in the distance. Utterly oblivious of other birds around him, undisturbed, in fact, by the splashing of jumping fish—mullet—nearby, he stood motionless, with patience unlimited, waiting for some unwary creature to stray within reach of his long neck and bill.

For most of the five months of his life Snowy had enjoyed pleasant weather. There had been a rainstorm when he was a nestling, but in among the mangrove leaves and shielded by his parent it had been an almost agreeable experience. Later, when he was on his own, summer storms on two occasions had driven him to the shelter of the nearest trees. He got wet, and wet feathers are exceedingly discomforting, but he soon dried out and was none the worse.

Indeed, his friends the cormorants and anhingas, who dove underwater in pursuit of their prey and who did not have efficient oil glands like many other diving birds, suffered constantly from wet feathers. Snowy often saw them perched with wings outstretched, drying out. But now something more than just a wetting was in the offing.

Snowy and his companions were on a sandy beach on the shore of the bay. They had no gift of prescience that made them aware of what was coming. They did, however, feel a certain uneasiness.

A wind that had started early in the morning was steadily increasing. The day was heavily overcast and the birds could sense a new, and therefore disturbing, condition as the pressure of the atmosphere grew less and less.

By afternoon uneasiness was giving way to near panic. The overcast had turned almost black. The wind had become a gale. Gulls and terns were overhead, flying in circles, screaming imprecations at the elements. The wind howled back, drowning out their cries. The sky, normal haven for those with the gift of flight, was turning against them.

Shorebirds, world travelers, and intrepid fliers, were simply retreating inland. But the big, bulky pelicans, afraid to launch themselves in such a gale, were huddled on the beach. Some spread thmselves out, grotesquely flat on the sand, to keep from being blown away.

Although this was the shore of a sheltered bay, waves and spume were being blown up along the beach. In many places scores of little fish were left stranded. It was a measure of the birds' fears that the minnows flopped out their lives undisturbed. There was no thought of eating them.

Snowy, like the rest, was now more concerned with the elements than with hunger. Whatever was happening, it was a threat. The answer to such a threat was a familiar, tested shelter. This was the roosting place. But could they reach it? Could they fly at all in such a wind? The noise of the gale was overpowering.

The flock took to the air with some difficulty. Almost at once they were swept along the beach by the wind. Fortunately, their roosting island could be reached by quartering the wind, for to fly against it would have been impossible. Keeping as low as they could, just over the tops of the white caps, they reached the island.

They landed low among the mangrove roots. Quite a few herons of various kinds, some pelicans, cormorants, and anhingas already were on the island huddled in the roots and trees. But many birds were absent and only a few more managed to straggle in later. It had now become impossible to fly. In the air one went where the roaring wind commanded.

When Snowy landed among the mangrove roots, his first thought was to get something between him and the wind. The thick, matted roots seemed a logical wind break but all the places near him already were occupied by shivering birds.

The howl of the wind had now become so loud he could not hear their warning cries. He didn't have to. He knew there was no room for him here. Trespassing was still forbidden.

Reluctantly, but as it was to turn out luckily, Snowy climbed up higher into the trees. He stayed close to a large trunk and at last found a suitable perch where he could keep the trunk between him and the wind. Here he huddled down to await whatever might be in store for him.

Below were birds crouched among the roots. Above were birds like Snowy, swaying in the trees. Suddenly there was a cracking noise. A limb gave way to the wind and fell. Four herons were smashed into the muddy water. Flapping desperately in a futile attempt to get into the air, they were forced down by the wind and drowned.

Snowy looked back on the beach. The shorebirds had all gone inland now, seeking shelter along with the terns and many of the gulls. There were other gulls, however, trapped on the beach with the pelicans, afraid now to take to the air at all, or even to try to walk in such a blow.

Like the pelicans, many gulls simply lay on the ground. They did not, however, spread out their wings like the flattened, larger birds, but held them tightly together with their heads pointed windward and down like an anchor. Others let the wind roll them along the beach, hoping shelter might be reached that way.

Snowy's attention was soon drawn to a multitude of other birds, for the most part strange to him. They seemed tiny, some not much bigger than large insects. Many were gaily colored. All had one thing in common. They were being helplessly borne along by the roaring wind. They were *Warblers* and other little land birds, miles from the normal course of their annual fall trips south.

Suddenly the wind stopped. After the roar the silence seemed overpowering. The gulls and pelicans on the beach flew off inland. So did some of the birds on the island. Most, however, like Snowy, stayed. By now it was almost night and time to be roosting anyway.

The silence was now being filled by the cries of birds, birds Snowy had never seen before. They resembled gulls and terns but for the most part were smaller and darker. The wind was coming up again and these birds were desperately struggling against it, seeking to fly directly into the wind toward the sea. These were oceanic birds, *Petrels* and *Shearwaters*, who came to land only at nesting time or, as now, in the eye of a hurricane. For days they had been traveling in this eye. But now that it had reached land, they were frantically trying to get out of it, back to the open ocean where their livelihoods lay. Few were going to make it. Most would perish in alien environments inland.

The wind was roaring again as loudly as ever. Snowy clung to his perch. Below and around him there seemed to be one vast mud flat. What, a few hours before, had been Florida Bay, was now almost empty of water. Then Snowy heard another roar, above that of the wind.

The water was coming back, in the form of a twelve-foot wave. Violence and destruction came with it. Snowy could feel the mangroves shake when the wave hit the island. He managed with difficulty to hold his perch. Some birds above him were not so lucky. Many were shaken loose and blown helplessly away by the wind. And most of those below him were sucked into the wave and drowned. Once again, as in the alligator-owl attack, Snowy was lucky to have been in the middle of the roost.

The mangroves had now lost virtually all their leaves and many of their limbs. But Snowy and the other survivors clung on. They could see a porpoise and a huge sea turtle being swept inland with the debris in the wave.

At last the winds started to diminish. Almost at once the rains came. Now almost shelterless, the birds were drenched. Through the long night they clung, cold, wet, and anxious. They would be helpless against a predator. They needn't have worried. Predator as well as prey was solely concerned with living out the storm.

Dawn came at last. There was no sun yet, but by spreading their wings the birds managed to achieve a measure of dryness. There were no enemies about and normality was returning. It brought with it what was normal: hunger.

One old bird of the sadly depleted little flock gave a cry and took to the air. Snowy and the others followed. Below them was a devastated world. Palms had lost their tops, mangroves were bare, and flats and beaches were littered with debris.

Death was everywhere. They saw the body of a white ibis impaled by a branch against which it had been blown. Other bodies were caught in forks of trees. A turkey vulture had died that way.

But when the flock landed at the edge of the water, the birds found even the storm was not without some blessing. All about them were little fish, shrimps, and other creatures, freshly dead or trapped in shallow pools.

The famished birds were soon glutted. And then at last the sun broke through. For hours they stood on the beach, drying, preening their feathers, dozing, and sunbathing. When the afternoon grew late, because they did not know of any place else that was better they returned to their leafless roost. Tomorrow they would find better quarters.

Some other birds, white ibis, Louisiana and little blue herons had also come back to roost, and in the morning the assorted flock, after feeding in the still bountiful pools, took off to seek a safer haven. They flew inland, north. For miles they could see debris, leafless trees, dead birds and other animals, all evidences of the storm. Finally they turned west toward the area of the inland waters and gulf islands that Snowy knew so well.

Only the edge of the storm had hit this area and here, still south of Snowy's homeland among the so-called Ten Thousand Islands, they found an unoccupied mangrove island that was suitable for roosting.

Tired after the flight, the flock descended and after preening fell asleep. They had survived a hurricane and found a new territory that would sustain them for a time.

VII

Snowy was now six months old. He had acquired a lot of confidence in himself. His plumage was not quite as sleekly white as that of the older birds, his yellow feet were not as bright, and his legs had juvenile bits of greenishness instead of being solidly black. But generally he looked just like his seniors.

In this he and the Louisiana herons were very different from the young little blue herons and white ibis with whom they had traveled from the storm area. Young little blues would be a dull white all their first year, in contrast to the blue and maroon of the older birds, and young white ibis were a mottled brown for their first year.

There was no mistaking these birds for adults, and they were easily kept in the subordinate positions that befitted the younger generation. Snowy and the young Louisianas, however, not only looked more like adults but sometimes they also acted that way.

Other birds had joined the group since their arrival, and while they all roosted together, they now usually traveled and fed in flocks of their own kind. Snowy decided one morning that he would take a day off from his flock and, on his own, see what hunting he could find.

From the air he had often seen the white beaches of the outer islands, lazily washed by the gulf surf. He had seen birds there but he had never visited the beaches himself. Now he was going to find out what they offered.

His more natural feeding places were the sheltered bays and estuaries or the inland fresh-water marshes and swamps. And he had no sooner landed on the beach than he realized the birds here were different from the ones to which he was accustomed. The same gulls and terns circled overhead but, at first at least, he saw no waders like himself, and the shorebirds seemed of a different sort.

Most numerous were flocks of small gray and white birds with black bills and legs that scampered out after each wave, plunged their bills rapidly up and down in the moist sand, and retreated in unison, like dancers, as the next wave came in. These were sanderlings, similar to but a little larger than the tiny sandpipers Snowy was used to seeing on the mud flats.

Occasionally, later, he would see sanderlings in the inland feeding grounds, but in general they seemed to prefer the beaches. Also finding nourishment in the seemingly sterile sand were some larger birds with brownish-gray backs, white underparts, and black aprons around the neck. Ruddy *Turnstones* were finding tiny animals farther back on the beach under shells or in patches of seaweed. Also in this area were the squattish black-bellied plovers Snowy was used to seeing inland, and out in the surf with the sanderlings were much bigger birds, the long-billed, noisy *Willets*.

Snowy tentatively probed into the sand with his bill. There must be food there. But he soon gave it up. These shorebirds might be equipped to snare prey out of the sand. Snowy was not. He was about to leave the beach altogether and forever when, far down the shore, he saw another egret like himself standing in the surf and, out in slightly deeper water, a long-legged great blue heron.

Imitation being the key to learning, Snowy too waded out in the surf. It was quite calm after the winds of the recent storm. Like the other herons he had seen, Snowy adopted the "stand and wait" technique. Then he discovered that food could be obtained on the beaches after all. Little schools of minnows were venturing into the surf to feed on the almost invisible organic life of the sea edge. Deftly Snowy seized one of the little fish and, despite its frantic struggles, worked it around until he could get its head into his bill first and swallow it. Before long another school came along and Snowy seized another morsel. Soon he had fed enough so he could walk back up on the dry beach to rest and preen.

He awoke from a half doze to see a man and a woman walking up the beach toward him.

Since they had invaded his home on the Key and put the metal tag around his leg that still sometimes annoyed him, Snowy had seen these Lords of the Earth only at considerable distance. In some places, when he was feeding on mud flats with other birds, he had seen them on dikes, peering at him and other birds through what looked like large extra eyes that they held up in front of their faces. Then, too, at his first roosting place away from the Key, when he and other birds were arriving in the evenings, he had often seen people standing across the water staring in the same way.

But these had been people at a distance. Now the two walking up the beach were getting close. Snowy was nervous. With his usual warning, *awrk . . awrk!*, he flew up and circled out over the water.

The people paid no attention. Neither did the other birds. Some gulls were resting on the beach. They didn't move until the people were only a few feet away and then the birds just flew lazily up the beach a short distance. The little shorebirds scampered along the sand ahead of the people, not even bothering to take to the air.

The man and woman turned inland and disappeared into a large shelter set back from the beach. On either side Snowy could see more of these houses, and he noticed that in front of some in the distance people were sitting in the sand.

Snowy went back to his roosting place that afternoon, joined by the other egret he had seen fishing in the surf. In the morning he went with the flock to the mud flats but, as the days went on, when the tide was high inland and the water calm in the gulf, Snowy would return to the beach to hunt minnows in the surf.

Like the other birds there, he grew less and less afraid of the people. They never seemed to bother him, or even to make threatening gestures—except on one occasion.

This came about, really, because of another bird, a great blue heron. One day Snowy saw a man standing out in the surf. He held a long rod from which a thin line extended far out into the deep. Suddenly the rod began to bend violently. The man could be seen winding in the line and walking up on the shore.

Then, at the end of the line, flopping and struggling through the surf, he pulled in a Spanish mackerel eighteen inches long. He took the fish off the line, threw it onto the sand behind him, returned to the water, and threw out the line again.

At this point Snowy saw the great blue. He had been resting farther back on the beach. Now, silently, majestically, he was striding toward the mackerel flopping its life out on the sand. Just as he seized the fish in his long, strong bill, the man turned and saw him. With a yell, still clinging to his rod, he ran toward the heron.

It did not seem possible that the bird could get airborne with such a load, but he did. With his great wings flapping, his neck and head forced downward by the weight of his loot, his long legs sticking out behind, the great blue managed to fly just over the sand down the beach.

The man gave up the chase and returned to his fishing. In the distance, the big heron carried the mackerel out to the surf, carefully washed the sand off of it, and after some intricate maneuvering to get the mackerel's head in first, he succeeded in swallowing it, or most of it. With the tail still protruding from his bill, the contented heron stalked back to the upper part of the beach to await digestion of the head so he could get the rest of it down.

Snowy looked on. He could never hope to swallow a fish like that. He had seen these great blue herons catch and swallow rodents and small birds, including those furtive marsh birds, the *Rails*, that he couldn't handle either. But one never knew, and anything that might serve as food was not to be overlooked. So, thereafter, on subsequent visits to the beach when the big heron was not around and the territory was open, Snowy kept a careful eye on any man he saw fishing in the surf.

Once he did see another man throw a fish back on the sand and leave it unattended. But it was another large one and, regretfully, Snowy had to pass it up. This man, however, was taking struggling little animals out of a tin can and hooking them onto the end of his line before he threw the line back in the water.

The can was setting well back on the beach. The man was in the surf, some distance away. Silently Snowy walked over to investigate. He peered into the can and to his amazement saw swimming about in that tiny pool of water half a dozen large luscious shrimps. They were larger than the crustaceans Snowy was able to catch on the mud flats. And seizing them in the narrow confines of the can was ridiculously easy! Snowy could scarcely believe his good fortune. In fact he was so engrossed and overjoyed that he almost came to grief.

He had two shrimps down and had just seized a third when he heard the man running toward him. Just in time, still clinging to that final shrimp, he flew off down the beach. The man had saved half his bait.

On another occasion, from the beach Snowy saw a large flock of both laughing and ring-billed gulls, calling excitedly and flying about some half mile offshore. Pelicans and cormorants were in the water below them. Many gulls were hovering just over the surface. Flying up a little, Snowy could see that there were small fish leaping below them being seized by the hungry birds.

Snowy arrived at the scene of this activity along with two boatloads of men. They started throwing lines into the water and pulling in large, struggling fish. It was a school of bluefish, jacks, and mackerel driving the little fish to the surface.

While it lasted, the excitement was intense. The gulls, who ordinarily cannot catch live fish without such help, were screaming in their frenzied greed. Pelicans were scooping up the little fish in their big pouches, not bothering to dive. The men were yelling to each other as they struggled with the big fish on their lines.

For Snowy this was a new kind of feeding but somehow he managed to adapt himself to it readily. Almost always before he had stood with feet firmly planted as he seized his prey. He had caught butterflies and other insects while flying but that had been accidental. They had simply come within reach and they were easy to swallow.

Now, out over this deep water, he had to hover with his wings and strike down at the elusive prey, while at the same time maintaining himself in the air. For he could not land in the water like a gull or pelican. The first few strikes at the little fish jumping below him were unsuccessful. He missed. But soon he managed to catch one, bring his head up, and swallow it. After that it was easier and he enjoyed a fine feeding.

Suddenly it was over. The big fish quit the hunt, the little fish sank to safer depths. Snowy flew back to the beach to rest and preen before returning to the roost for the night.

VIII

EARLY one morning Snowy saw a strange performance.
Indirectly it would send him traveling again.

He was hunting in the shallows of a tidal flat near a
small, sandy island. Other small herons and some white
ibis were nearby. Out in the deeper water were some
of the larger egrets. Shorebirds ran back and forth
along the waterline of the island.

There was a large shadow overhead. The birds started
up but it was only a great blue heron who soared down
slowly and landed on the island. The shorebirds scuttled
out of reach and Snowy edged away. He always gave
these huge cousins a respectful distance.

He had not seen one at close quarters for some time and he noticed that the great blue had changed in appearance. Not much but enough to be observed. The plumes standing back from his blue and white head were longer and a shinier black. The feathers over his breast stood out, longer and a brighter reddish brown.

Instead of stalking out into the deeper water in search of prey as he usually did, the big heron stayed on the island, preening. Soon another great blue appeared in the sky and soared down beside him. The two faced each other, wings half outspread, and began a stately, circular promenade. Soon another of the big birds joined them, then another, until there were a dozen or more on the island.

Some drew themselves up to their full four-foot height and, slowly flapping their outstretched wings, danced about in a circle. At times they would lunge at each other, stabbing out with their long, sharp bills.

Snowy and the other birds, who had stopped feeding to watch, moved a little farther away. Some of the big herons had not joined the dance. These were hens. They stood watching the display and the aggressive male gestures. Age-old urges were released within them. The hens began crouching down submissively, uttering low, coaxing croaks.

The dancers kept circling, but their recognition of this femaleness was, in turn, affecting them. Attitudes of belligerence were giving way to desire. Sometimes two would approach the same hen and lively, though never fatal, encounters might take place. Sometimes the hen would signify her preference and the rejected one would go seek elsewhere.

Thus, little by little, the birds formed into pairs. And, as each compact was made, two by two, they flew off

—all but one, a younger male. He was left standing in lonely, disconsolate grandeur on the island. But soon he seemed to forget the whole incident. He waded into the deeper water and started hunting. Other basic urges had to be fulfilled too.

Shorebirds soon returned to the island and Snowy and the others resumed their feeding. But Snowy felt restless. It had all released certain vague stirrings within him. He went back to the roost that night. In the morning, although he felt hunger, some stronger urge bade him return to the area of his origin.

He set off northward along the coast. As often happened when an individual flew out purposefully, others were stimulated to join him. So he made the flight with three other young egrets. It took two hours and by that time the urge that had brought him home was forgotten, submerged by the greater commands of the empty stomach.

Snowy led the little flock unhesitatingly to the flats where he had fed for the first time on his own. It was just as crowded as when Snowy had left some months before, but he was older and had developed some dominance of his own. He led his group close to some little blue herons who, when they saw that he meant business, grudgingly made room for them.

Snowy looked about and saw, out in the deeper water, many new birds he had never seen before. He was familiar with the rather plain-looking, brownish mottled duck that he had previously seen with her fluffy babies. Now her cousins had arrived from the north. There were hundreds of ducks of many different kinds. Most of the drakes were handsome, colorful, but all their mates were as drab as were both sexes of the stay-at-home mottled duck, which never migrated.

There was one of the new northern visitors that Snowy was going to find very useful. This discovery was made that very afternoon. The tide had come in and Snowy and the other waders were resting along the bank of a canal. The water was deep and, except in the rare instances when some aquatic creature would be careless enough to stray up to the surface close to the bank, little was to be gained by hunting here.

Half dozing in the sun, Snowy was startled to hear a great splashing commotion out in the middle of the canal. There he saw a dozen ducks, but ducks unlike any of the others. They were more gray than brown, with pale reddish heads, the feathers of which often stood up like crests, and their bills were exceedingly unducklike: long and almost as thin as Snowy's, although not as pointed as his.

It was their behavior, however, more than their appearance that had attracted Snowy's attention. And this was the cause of the commotion in the canal. Sometimes these birds would dive under the water like cormorants and anhingas, but often they simply chased little fish along the surface, running over the water with feet and wings splashing, seizing their prey in the long, thin bills. These were *Red-Breasted Mergansers*, females and young males. The old drakes seldom made the journey so far south.

Snowy was aware that a great many other wading birds, other egrets, herons, and ibis, most of them birds older and more experienced than he, were gathering along both banks of the canal. At once he realized why.

Little fish, desperately trying to escape the avid, fast-moving mergansers, were scurrying away. And away meant toward the shore. Here all the other birds were poised.

Snowy looked down and saw panic-stricken minnows coming toward him. Instantly he and the others along the banks were feasting on these escapees from the mergansers. As the ducks carried on their pursuit along the center of the canal, herons and ibis flew on along the banks, squabbling among themselves for positions just ahead of them. It was a fine feast, enough for all. And Snowy learned he could benefit as well as suffer from the acts of others.

That evening he went to his old roosting place on the big, outer island, the one in the marsh where he had spent his first nights away from the Key. It was still crowded with many different kinds of birds, but Snowy managed to assert himself enough to find a place. Perhaps, even with his growing dominance, he wouldn't have been able to, except that space had been left by the departure of many great blue herons. Snowy had witnessed their courting. They were now spending their nights on their nesting islands instead of at the communal roost. The great blues mostly nested earlier than the other herons, even while the days were still growing shorter.

As time went on Snowy fitted into the routine of his old haunts. He had plenty of companions of his own kind. They were usually out on the mud flats when the tide was low, at other times in the fresh-water inland marshes, and, occasionally, when the gulf was calm, one or two would try hunting in the surf.

Often now, when he would see a flock of mergansers, he would land nearby and many times he was able to secure little fish, shrimps, or other animals fleeing from these active ducks. As he got bolder he would sometimes fly out over the deeper water, right in front of the mergansers and, hovering as he had done that day over the school of fish in the gulf, snatch a minnow almost out of the duck's bill. The angry merganser would protest but he dared not challenge Snowy's longer, sharper beak.

Snowy learned, too, that he could benefit from other birds as well. He found that sometimes cormorants and anhingas, in their divings, would scare things toward him. And sometimes, standing quietly near where other herons or ibis were moving about, he was able to catch prey fleeing from them.

He learned also, however, that this sort of thing could work both ways. There was another new arrival from the north, a bird quite different from any other. It was about half Snowy's size, much shorter and stockier, blue and white with long blue feathers forming a crest on the head. The female, with a rusty belt around her middle, was more handsome than the male.

These were *Kingfishers* and, as their name implied, they were experts at their craft. This Snowy was going to discover to his great annoyance. He was hunting in a shallow marsh one day and not having much luck. The water was clear and the bottom hard, so he tried the "disturb and pursue" technique. He ran about energetically. His yellow feet flashing along the bottom startled many little minnows out from hiding places in the short grass. But when Snowy started to reap the reward for this effort, he was in for a surprise.

He had not noticed a kingfisher perched on a nearby

limb. Just as Snowy struck at the first minnow he heard a swish and a splash in front of him. Up came the kingfisher with Snowy's hoped-for prey struggling in his strong bill. Snowy cried out in angry protest. The kingfisher simply swallowed the fish and, as Snowy started to lunge at another, dove down in front of him again. He was always wily and quick enough to elude Snowy's bill and in the end succeeded in getting most of the fish that had been scared up. In the future Snowy would not try that method of hunting if he saw a kingfisher nearby.

The days and weeks rolled on. Snowy seemed to have all the ingredients of contentment. He had his own kind around him. He was reasonably free from predation by his enemies. He was managing to secure enough food. But he was not content.

The days were now getting longer and warmer. This increased light and heat had begun to work mysterious glandular changes in Snowy's body.

He was conscious of vague stirrings and restlessness. When he preened himself now, he found that old feathers had been replaced by new, longer, and finer ones on his neck, head, and back. He admired these plumes and preened them carefully. But for all their gleaming beauty, they were dull and short compared to the new plumage now being acquired by Snowy's older companions. He could see on them long, wispy plumes, flowering at the ends in an extravagance of the finest, whitest filaments.

There were other changes taking place too. The older birds, especially the males, were becoming decidedly less friendly. In fact, sometimes for no reason at all, they were downright hostile.

One afternoon Snowy descended to one of his favorite mud flats. As usual, there were birds of several different kinds already feeding there and Snowy landed among some other small egrets of his own kind. He started hunting next to an older bird but far enough away to show that he respected the other's domain and would not trespass. This was the rule. It had always been accepted before.

But now Snowy sensed that something was wrong. He looked up just in time. The bird was crouched, facing him. His feathers, especially his crest and the long new plumes about his head and neck, were extended, waving in the wind. His wings were half spread out. His eyes bulged and the skin between his eyes and his beak had changed from yellow to red.

He gave a hoarse, aggressive cry. *Aard . . aard!* Then he lunged at Snowy. The younger bird had no desire for a fight. Just barely avoiding the angry bill, Snowy half flew, half ran, to another part of the flat. In doing so, he had to duck around another old bird who also had his gorgeous new feathers ruffled and his wings outspread.

This one did have a desire for a fight. Just as Snowy got out of the way the two older birds crashed together, crying and jabbing viciously at each other. Back and forth they tumbled until the second bird decided he had had enough. He broke off the engagement and flew to another area.

Tempers quickly cooled. Only a few feathers, lost by both birds remained on the mud to indicate a battle had taken place. In the next few days Snowy was going to witness quite a few of these encounters. They always appeared vicious, even deadly, but in the end no one ever got really hurt.

With the lengthening days Snowy noticed another change in habits. Quite a few of the older birds were leaving the feeding grounds in the afternoon earlier than usual. Yet they didn't go back to the roosting place. In fact, each evening when Snowy returned there he found fewer and fewer companions. There was no longer the problem of crowding. He could perch and sleep now almost wherever he wanted.

One afternoon, instead of returning to the roost, he joined one of the little flocks that was leaving early. Once they started he didn't need them to guide him. Suddenly he knew where they were going. He even separated a little from them and, without hesitation, flew directly to the Key, the little mangrove island where he had come into the world.

What a sight greeted him! All the different birds were gathering. They were flying about or were perched on trees or bushes, all strikingly colorful in their new plumages—blue herons, white egrets, bronze ibis, grayish night herons, brown pelicans, black cormorants, and anhingas.

And what noise! All were more active, louder than Snowy had ever seen or heard before. Fights and pursuits, name callings, warnings, and self-advertisements were going on all over the Key in all the different languages.

Some of the larger birds, the great blue herons and some of Snowy's closer relatives, the big egrets, were already flattened down on nests incubating eggs. They seemed quietly annoyed at all the confusion around them.

As usual Snowy was pulled toward his own kind. In this case he was going to regret it. He was soon to learn that the other species would seldom bother him or, in fact, pay much attention to him. Not so with his fellow egrets. Snowy came down onto a branch of a mangrove not far from two or three of them. He didn't stay long. All this was well-defended private property. Almost at once the nearest old male bird, feathers raised, took off from his perch and lunged at Snowy. This was more deadly than the attack on the mud flat. The gleaming sharp bill meant business. Snowy got away just in time.

He flew off a little distance and came to rest, this time safely, on a limb already bowed down by the weight of a perching pelican. The old pelican paid him not the slightest heed. Snowy, preening his new plumes, looked back at the birds he had left.

There were half a dozen, perched in conspicuous places. Each was trying to outdo the others in calling attention to himself. *Aard . . aard!*, they would cry. Sometimes there was an even louder, harsher call with a liquid, gurgling finish. *Ar-ogle . . ar-ogle!*

Every now and then one would fly up from his perch. He would be joined by others, all circling about in a sort of ritualistic flight. Snowy finally joined one such excursion, since everyone seemed to be welcome, and in this case no one bothered him.

There were other young birds like himself in the group, birds just less than a year old, whose first new plumage lacked the length and brilliance of the older birds. As the little group flew in circles over the Key, the stirrings that had been released within Snowy became more demanding. What he wanted above all was some place he could call his own. How he longed to land down on one of those branches among the others, take possession of his own territory, and chase away any other bird who came too close. But the memory was still fresh of how he had escaped, just barely, that deadly bill. Someday he would own a place on this Key. But he didn't dare challenge the older, gaudier birds right now. He kept on flying.

Below he could see more of the colony's activities. There seemed to be little segregation of the species. Mixed in with some of his own kind and with each other, he saw little blue and Louisiana herons perched on conspicuous limbs, calling loudly, advertising themselves much as the little egrets were doing. There was a great deal of individual variation in all this. No two birds, even of the same species, seemed to do it in exactly the same way. Some were calling, bending, bowing up and down with such exuberance that it seemed they would topple over. Others were more restrained, almost sedate about it.

Snowy had only a few minutes to watch all this from the sky. Soon the flight was over. The little group swooped down, the birds landed back at their original perches, and the leader renewed his warning to all within earshot that this was his property.

By now the sun was setting. Things began to quiet down. Snowy had no thought of returning to his regular roosting place. Certainly he had no desire to venture out alone into skies where owls or other predators might be lurking, and there was no sign of any flock about to leave. Roosting would have to take place where he was, so Snowy settled on his limb, slowly relaxed, and dropped off to sleep.

He awoke at dawn, hunger now obliterating the stirring he had felt the day before. Most of the other birds, except some already nest-building or setting, must have felt the same, for as the sun rose large flights started for the various feeding grounds.

Snowy joined one and landed with the others on a tidal flat. The hunting was good and soon his immediate hunger was appeased. Usually he would now preen, rest, and then go seek more prey elsewhere. Instead he found himself heading back toward the Key.

He was careful this time to land on top of a mangrove near the outer edge, not getting close enough to anger other birds. The excitement now was even more intense than the day before. Birds of all species were crying more loudly, fighting more often, flying about noisier than ever. Snowy, of course, was mainly interested in his own kind and was startled to see an old male egret in a posture unlike anything seen before.

The bird, in full and beautiful white plumage, had his neck strained so far back his head was almost over his tail. His glistening black beak was pointed straight upward. He had the same look of anger Snowy had observed in the birds that had attacked him. Eyes bulged; skin by the beak was red; feathers, plumes, and crest were raised, and his usually bright yellow feet, gripping the branch, had turned coral-orange.

Keeping his head strained back and his beak pointed upward, the bird was bending his legs, pumping his head up and down. He uttered a new cry, louder and shriller: *waa . . aaa . . waa!*

Other birds seemed to be drawn, irresistibly, by this display. Snowy and half a dozen others flew over to perch in a circle around him, watching. At this the displaying bird seemed to get more furious than ever. He straightened out, lunged at the spectators until he drove them away.

By this time there were others, seemingly inspired by this first one, putting on similar displays although with some variations. So, birds driven away by one would simply fly to another tree or bush and perch around watching another performance until they were driven away again.

After a while Snowy grew tired and stopped to rest. He could see that some of the birds were refusing to be driven away or were returning when the other spectators had left. Gradually this behavior began to work changes in the displaying birds. They were recognizing signs of femaleness and reacting to it. They began to welcome hens. Sometimes if two hens stayed or returned, one of them would drive the other away.

Finally, only one would be left to watch and admire. Then, for this select audience, the performer would outdo himself. Snowy watched one.

Flinging himself into the air, bill still pointing upward now at a forty-five-degree angle, feathers and plumes outstretched to the fullest, the male circled up, up, up. The female below watched intently. Suddenly her suitor folded his wings, plummeted downward, tumbling over and over, and landed feet first on the branch beside her.

She did not leave. He was accepted. Soon the two flew off together, circling about, and returned to the territory he had staked out. There the alliance was consummated. Now they were a mated pair. In most, but not all, cases they would be faithful for the season, interested only in each other and a new generation.

These sights and sounds were intensifying the glandular changes in Snowy. From his remote perch he tried calling and posturing as he had seen the older birds do. *Waa . . aa . . waa!* No one paid any attention. He strained to curl his neck back over his tail. His plumes were too short to make an effective display.

He flew about the colony seeking company, but whenever he tried to land near others of his kind he was summarily chased away. No one wanted this property-less upstart.

Despite his rejection, Snowy could not stay away from the Key. He had roosted there again and left at dawn. As soon as his immediate hunger was appeased he headed back.

Courting, lovemaking, nest-building were now going on at an ever-increasing pace, and other birds were joining the colony. The tide was quite low. Out on some exposed flats nearby, a pair of big brown pelicans stood placidly gazing at each other. The male spread his wings and marched ponderously around the object of his attention. Without much more ado, these, the least demonstrative birds of the colony, flew off together.

Up near a half-constructed nest high in a white mangrove, a black male cormorant stood. He bowed to his mate, who was standing on the nest. With wings open, neck outstretched and swollen, he walked on the branches around her, opening and closing his bill. She stepped off the nest and they sat together, caressing each other with bills and necks.

Nearby a pair of the cormorant's close relative, the anhinga, sat together. Her brownish neck and breast lay against his black ones. He puffed out a pouch on his upper throat and cried out in his rough, gutteral language of love. The two twined their long, snakelike necks about each other.

High on the top of a red mangrove a Louisiana heron was showing off. In his nuptial dress he had many colors. Long white plumes waved up from his blue head and back, the buff-colored feathers on his lower neck stood out above his glistening white breast. He was bowing elegantly to an admiring hen on the branch below. Daintily he danced along the bough, wings half spread, bowing and weaving until he reached her. Their mating pact was consummated then and there.

Other Louisianas and some of the delicate blue and maroon little blue herons, perched on conspicuous limbs, were busy advertising themselves and their property. They struck poses similar to the ones of Snowy's kind: neck pulled far back, bill pointing upward, head waving.

A pair of black-crowned night herons, perched near-by, were showing off intently to each other. Both had their white plumes raised above their black and white heads. Grayish breast feathers and dark blue back feathers were ruffled and raised. A third black-crown, another hen, landed next to them. The displaying female drove her off. The male then approached closer and the two caressed with their bills.

Near the center of the Key, in a thick bush, were several pairs of glossy ibis. Their long downcurved bills and rusty bronze plumes were gleaming. They were the noisiest of all, making a din that could be heard above all the other multi-species crying. The males were expanding and contracting the pouches in their necks while the females looked on admiringly.

Many of the larger birds of Snowy's own heron family, the great blue herons and the glistening white, larger egrets, had already settled property rights, chosen mates, and started housekeeping. In fact, one great blue heron nest, carefully guarded by one of the parents, already contained three downy youngsters. They were jumping up and down, waving their little stumps of wings, screaming for food.

Slightly below, in the same white mangrove tree, an American egret was setting, her long white plumes hanging over the edges of the nest. Suddenly she let out a gurgling cry. Her mate had just landed nearby and, wings outspread, plumage erect, he danced along the branch toward her. She rose from the nest, her own plumes raised. They called to each other as he approached. He bowed and caressed her with his bill. After a little she flew off to the feeding grounds. Slowly he settled down to take his turn at providing the warmth needed to keep the lives growing inside the pale blue eggs.

There was a somber backdrop to it all. Overhead crows and vultures were beginning to circle. The piratical frigate birds, when they had finished their own nesting down south, would soon join them. There would never be a moment without a menace close at hand.

The noises and activities within the colony were being enlivened by many a raucous squabble. Nest-building was under way in earnest and, as always, building material was at a premium. Remnants of the nests of the year before were being dismantled. Twigs and small branches were being picked up from the ground, out of the water, or broken off dead limbs.

Some birds, unable to find anything that suited them on the Key, were flying the mile and a half to the mainland and back with the needed supplies, making one trip after another. The gathering of this material was being done mostly by the males, and few sticks were

obtained without fending off a would-be robber. In
fact, even after a stick was carefully woven into the
nest it might be snatched out by some other eager
builder. Naturally, all this occasioned many a noisy
dispute.

When the male finally obtained sole possession of a
branch or twig, whether by pilfering or otherwise, he
would bear it in triumph to his waiting mate. Bowing,
with wings outspread and plumes extended, he would give
it over to her. She would carefully fit it into its place
while he went off to join again in the noisy struggle to
obtain another piece or make the long flight to the
mainland.

The birds were adept at this work. Even the pelicans
with their big bills, and hindered by their monstrous
pouches, could deftly snatch up a twig and weave it
into a nest. In most cases within two days the flimsy
but serviceable platforms that all the birds constructed
would be completed. Green leaves would then be pulled
from the mangroves to serve as lining.

Completed nests had to be guarded carefully. If left
unattended long they would be sure to be dismantled
by robbers, and all the work would have to be done
again. In fact, from now on a constant guard had to be
maintained to protect first the building material, then
the eggs, and finally, most precious, the young.

Snowy, like most of the younger birds, was a spectator
rather than a participant in all this activity. Suddenly
he felt himself caught up in longings older than his race,
longings that could not be denied.

He was watching his own kind, the other little egrets.
He saw one female drive another away in order to be

with a displaying male by herself. Swiftly, Snowy flew after the departing, rejected hen.

He landed beside her, not knowing exactly what he intended or how he intended to go about it. She decided matters for him. Viciously she jabbed at him, driving him back. Even if she could not have the propertied, displaying male she wanted, there was no urge within her to submit to this intrusive youngster.

It was scarcely the reception Snowy had hoped for. Dejected, he withdrew, another lesson learned. Mates were not to be secured by bypassing established procedures.

Looking about, he saw another young male like himself. But this one had a mate! Proudly he was standing by a nest. This couple was, as a matter of fact, a little ahead of most of the other small herons. She was already setting on eggs. Her young mate was standing nearby ready to relieve her.

Snowy accepted the favored status of the older, more dominant birds. But why should this youngster have everything—his own territory, a mate, a family coming on—and Snowy have nothing?

Angrily he flew at the youngster, intent on driving him away. But instead of one, he found himself facing two antagonists. The old female rose from her eggs and joined her mate in driving Snowy off.

As a matter of fact, this young male had achieved a mate in his first year by luck. Her original spouse, presumably the victim of some predator, had failed to return from a feeding trip. She desperately needed a replacement if her eggs were not to be lost when she left them to feed herself. He had simply happened by at the critical time.

There would be no such accident to help Snowy.

Perforce his young urges were subsiding. In another year his desires would be stronger, his dominance and attractiveness greater. Until then he must be patient.

He returned to the branch upon which he had been roosting. Conflicting urges were now stirring within him. On the one hand he wanted to stay here, on the Key where he had been hatched. If he were to participate in the process of procreation, it should be here, his home. Young birds were needed around the colony to serve as replacements for vanished mates.

On the other hand, the same chemical changes in Snowy's glands that had given him his new plumes, that had released within him the desire for territory and a mate, that had given him the temporary power to procreate, these changes had other commands as well.

As far back as biological memory could reach, many of his kind had traveled when the days began to get longer and warmer. The urge to stay at the nesting Key was frustrated. A new urge, a migratory pull, was taking its place.

Snowy would go north.

IX

It was now mid-April, a little late in the year for migration. Many of the northern visitors had already started their return trips, mostly in small flocks of their own kind. Many of Snowy's generation, year-old egrets like himself, young Louisiana and little blue herons had gone with them. The young little blues were a strange-looking group at this time. Some still had their all-white juvenile plumage, some had molted into their blue dress, and others were in the halfway stage, speckled blue and white.

Food had been relatively plentiful this year, however,

so quite a few of the old northerners, the regular migrants, were still in the area. Snowy started feeding with these visitors rather than with the nesting birds coming out from the colony. He resumed going back to his old roosting place each evening and made no more visits to the Key.

Before long he had attached himself to a flock of twenty or so other little white herons, mostly old birds from the north. This group was dominated by one old male. He made no gesture of welcome to Snowy, but since the young bird was careful to keep a proper distance in feeding and roosting and made no move to challenge the leadership, the older birds suffered Snowy to remain.

It wasn't always easy. These northern birds were a little later in getting their new plumage than were those of the south. Many were just undergoing the glandular changes that brought the brilliant feathers along with the need to show them off and to prove superiority. Snowy was often hard put to avoid being driven clear away by old males anxious to demonstrate their aggressiveness.

But he persisted, and finally one afternoon, when they had taken off from an inland marsh where they had been feeding, the leader headed in a new direction. Instead of west across the sound and back to the roosting place, he turned north. A few of the birds dropped back and headed for the roost. They just didn't want to leave at this time. But most stayed with the leader. So did Snowy.

The old bird led them up high into the sky. Snowy could not remember ever having been so far up. It began to get dark and he could see man-made lights of cities twinkling below and the more familiar lights of the stars above.

Higher and higher they went. The old bird kept shifting his course, as though unsure of himself. Finally Snowy could feel a steady wind behind him, helping him on his way. At this the leader appeared satisfied. Steadily, hour after hour, the little flock rode the air current into the north.

This was no simple trip looking for new feeding or roosting places. These birds meant business. They were flying fast, they knew just where they were going, and there would be no stopping until they got there.

All night they flew. Snowy had never made as long a flight before. He was strong, healthy, and well fed, with lots of fat, but he began to tire. By the time dawn came his muscles were aching, his wings seemed to weigh twice as much as usual. Still there was no rest in sight. On and on they flew. Only the helping wind from behind enabled Snowy to maintain the pace.

He looked down in the growing light. What he saw determined that whatever happened, no matter how long this was to go on, he must keep flying even if he died of exhaustion. He could not leave the flock.

For what he saw was an utterly alien, unfriendly land. It was one into which he would not dare venture, certainly not alone. Far off to his right he could see endless open, turbulent water beyond a thin white beach. But this was not the kind of beach he was used to at home, one lapped by gentle waves providing surf in which he could hunt. This beach was being battered by long, rolling combers in which Snowy could not have survived and in which there would probably be no food for him even if he could.

Inland, directly below him, instead of the mangroves
and lagoons, the ponds and marshy fields, he saw only
starkness and aridity. Instead of the few houses for men
he was used to seeing—and avoiding—here there were
thousands with no spaces in between. Above them was
a tangle of poles and wires. Smoke billowed up in a hundred places. He forgot his aching muscles. There was
no stopping here.

Soon they were passing over more open country. It
was scarcely less forbidding. Only here and there were
there dots of green. Dry fields, tall towers with wires
strung between them, long ribbons of gray on which sped
dark objects (automobiles) moving in both directions
faster than Snowy, with all his efforts, could fly, gleaming parallel bars of steel along which moved other long
snakelike objects, trains in a marshaling yard—these
alien sights were all Snowy could see.

He longed for a glimpse of tidal flats or green marshes.
At last, ahead, he did see water. Snowy wanted to start
a descent, but the flock made no move toward coming
down. Soon he knew why.

They were passing over a river, but not a river like
Snowy had ever seen. Instead of open or grassy banks
along which one might feed, there were stone embankments. Pilings and piers jutted out into the deeper water.
In the middle, instead of cormorants and mergansers to
drive fish to the shallows, there were big flat boats,
barges, and floating debris. There were men everywhere.
There were no birds.

The flock flew on. At last they came to some tidal
flats. Here once there must have been a feeding ground
for thousands of birds. What they saw below them now,
however, was a huge network of wires, power lines
strung from tall, steel monstrosities that would have

made descent difficult. But no descent was contemplated. Below the wires, instead of open flats where animal prey might be found, smoke fumed up from garbage dumps, the burning offal of man's society. There were huge piles of abandoned automobiles. Inland were the huge chimneys of factories from which rose dull gray smoke. It was fortunate for Snowy and his companions that their olfactory senses were rudimentary. They could not get the stench. But their eyes smarted from the pollution in the air through which they flew.

Over this horror, the leader turned the flock inland. They passed the factories, a network of roads and houses, and soon Snowy could see ahead an open expanse. And here were reeds and cattails similar to those Snowy had seen in the south! There was grass and willow trees. They seemed a little brown and dry, but it must mean water and food.

At last the leader started down. They passed over a narrow canal and then, suddenly, the leader seemed bewildered. He started circling, crying out. The other birds joined in the cries. Snowy saw they were over what looked like a marsh. But there was scarcely any water. Just a pool here and there and the canal.

At the end of this he saw a big machine scooping up dirt. It was making the canal deeper and what water was left in the marsh was draining off down this canal.

One thing was certain. The birds had no choice as to what to do. They were exhausted. Keeping a safe distance from the machine and the man inside it, they landed on the newly turned up bank of the canal. Snowy was so thankful for the opportunity to rest his aching muscles that at first he was conscious of no other motivation. He stood and rested.

It wasn't long, however, before he began thinking

about food. He looked about him. In the willows nearby were some old nests. Although smaller, this had been a heronry, a breeding colony like his on the Key. Old nests were here, but no birds.

This had been the home to which the little flock had been so determined to return. Snowy looked at the birds around him. They stood on the bank without purpose, long plumes drooping.

Instead of the bustle of a nesting colony, releasing basic urges, here there was nothing. Who would want to claim worthless territory? No families could be raised here. There was no food for demanding, hungry youngsters. The birds stood in tired bewilderment.

Familial urges were behind Snowy for this year; now his stomach was demanding that he start to forage. Without thinking he came close to the leader, almost bumping him. Snowy started away, fearing an attack, but the old bird paid no attention. His dominance was gone. Snowy started working his way along the edge of the canal.

The full measure of his predicament had not yet dawned on him. The leadership that had brought him here had been abdicated. The flock that had given him safety was breaking up. He was about to be alone with a thousand miles of hostile land between him and home.

It was midafternoon and there were two immediate imperatives: food and a roosting place.

In regard to the first, Snowy had a bit of luck. He started down the bank toward the water when he saw a movement. He had never yet hunted on dry land, but quick as a flash he struck. He came up with a five-inch animal struggling in his bill, frantically waving arms and legs, head and tail.

Whatever it was, Snowy wasn't going to lose it. He beat the animal against the ground until the struggling ceased. Then he walked down to the water, carefully washed the dirt off his victim, and swallowed it. It was his first lizard, enough to sustain him for some time.

This was fortunate, for Snowy was going to find little else in the drained-out marsh. He walked along the edge of the canal. The water was muddy. If there had been anything under the surface Snowy couldn't have seen it anyway. He walked on, finding nothing.

From across the canal he heard a cheerful, musical call. *Okalee . . . okalee!* There, epaulets on his shoulders gleaming, was a *Red-Winged Blackbird*. Snowy felt a little better. This was a familiar friend at home.

Looking down the canal, Snowy saw a relative he knew. He was a bluish-green bird about two-thirds Snowy's size, with shorter legs, and a red neck and dark head crest. He was a little green heron, like the even more furtive *Bitterns*, an antisocial, or at least nonsocial, member of the heron family. Snowy had often seen them at home, usually alone and often feeding along canals like this one. They seldom came near the social herons like Snowy.

Anyway, it proved there was some life left in the dry marsh. But these birds were of little help in showing Snowy where food might be found. The redwing was busy securing little insects around a willow tree. The green heron was hunting in his own peculiar way. He was out in the middle of the canal where the water was clearer, his feet clinging to a log while his body and short neck reached down and out just over the water.

He was utterly motionless, waiting for some tiny creature to swim within reach.

Snowy had seldom been successful poised that way
over deeper water. Nor had he hunted inland for insects
after the manner of the blackbird. But he was in a new
land and he would have to learn new methods. In time
he would. After all, he already had mastered one important new technique—catching a lizard.

Hunger probably would have compelled him to try
other new methods at once had it not been for the lizard. With that in his stomach the desire became para-
mount to fulfill his other immediate need, a safe place to
sleep.

He looked about him and suddenly became frightened.
He was alone! The birds he had traveled with had vanished. Some had gone off searching for any remnant of
the colony they had known the year before; others had
decided to explore other marshes they knew about in
the neighborhood.

Snowy, who knew nothing of the neighborhood, had
no idea where to look for them. He was utterly alone
in a strange land. There were not even any of his social
relatives in sight, little blue and Louisiana herons, or the
bigger egrets. He could feel almost as secure roosting
with them as with his own kind.

He flew up, circling about in the hope of finding
companions of some kind. He caught sight of a white
speck in the distance and flew toward it. It was another
little egret standing at the edge of a tiny pool. Snowy
soared down and landed nearby.

The birds looked at each other. The stranger was a
youngster like himself. Snowy advanced toward him. He
retreated. So Snowy was the dominant one; he would

have to assume the leadership. There seemed to be no more food on the shores of this pond than there had been at the canal. Snowy took to the air again and this time the other bird followed him. He gave no indication of having a destination in mind. Obviously he knew of no roosting place, so Snowy headed for a clump of willows he saw in the distance.

The thin, sparse willow leaves did not offer the shelter Snowy was accustomed to in the larger-leafed mangroves, but the birds found perches as protected as possible. Snowy was now exhausted, having flown all the night before, so he made short work of his preening and soon fell asleep. It was not to be a restful night.

There was almost a full moon and many enemies were about. Once he was awakened by a terrifying cry he had heard before. *Hoohoo . . . hoohooaw.* Trembling, he shrank back under the branches. A barred owl was quite close.

Later he was awakened by a more immediate danger. Here there was no alligator below protecting the roost from four-footed tree climbers, or no yellowlegs, a tattler, to warn of peril. Snowy sensed rather than saw or heard anything. Then, in the moonlight, he caught the gleam of eyes. *Awrk . . awrk!* Snowy gave the warning of danger. A feral house cat, the enemy from which he had so narrowly escaped once before, was climbing up their tree.

Snowy remembered the cry of the owl. He dared not fly into that hazard even to escape this one. He backed away from the trunk making his way out onto smaller, less secure limbs that might not support the weight of the cat.

He looked at his companion, roused by Snowy's warning cry. The other bird seemed frozen with fright, hesitating whether to flee into the air or back away as Snowy was doing. Survival leaves little room for hesitation. There was a silent leap, an agonized cry. The cat was making his way back down the tree, his sharp teeth grasping the neck of the still crying, still struggling bird.

Now Snowy was alone. There was to be no more sleep for what was left of that night. He remained, trembling, on the outer limbs until, finally, dawn came. Even then he waited until it was light enough to ensure safety from other nocturnal enemies before leaving this unhappy roosting place.

Snowy's nature now demanded security, the security of a safer environment and the security of the companionship of others. But even before that, there were now the demands of hunger. He had had nothing to eat except that one lizard for thirty-six hours, during which he had flown a thousand miles.

When he left the willows, he ignored the unproductive water in the canals and little pond. He had seen the blackbird finding something on dry land. He would have to try that. He landed in a field of low grass and started walking very slowly, as he often did while hunting in shallow water, peering intently down into the grass. Every now and then he would detect a movement, but nothing he could see well enough for a strike.

Finally he tried another technique he had used in the water. He extended a yellow foot and, vibrating it, stirred the top of a clump of grass. Out jumped a fat insect, landing on another tuft of grass nearby. Now Snowy had his eyes fixed on his prey. He stalked, struck, and swallowed the struggling insect almost in one motion. It was a grasshopper.

Carefully Snowy went on hunting. Sometimes grass-hoppers or other insects flushed at his approach, some-times he roused them by stirring the grass. Sometimes he caught them as they leaped up, sometimes after he saw where they landed, and sometimes he missed altogether. But he caught enough so it wasn't long before he had his hunger under enough control so that the urge to find companions and a new locality took over.

He remembered the river he had crossed with the flock when they were flying north. It hadn't looked very promising but at least it was water. Despite his harvest of insects in the field, Snowy preferred to hunt with his feet wet.

He took to the air and flew south until he sighted the river. He was a little upstream from where he had crossed it before but still he could see no grassy banks or marshes. He turned and flew on up the river. There was no sign of any life whatever, except men.

Finally, beyond a stone embankment, he saw an open muddy flat. Except for some pilings it looked something like the mud flats he had fed on at home. There should be food here. He landed at the edge of the water just as a man came walking along the embankment. Since his association with them on the beaches, Snowy had lost much of his fear of these Lords of the Earth, and this man made no aggressive move. In fact he turned and ran back, motioning with his arm. He was joined by another man and the two stood staring at the white bird shining against the black of the mud.

Snowy, meanwhile, was taking stock. There were some unsightly objects that he had seen before on the beaches: old tin cans, bottles, and other litter. But here it was infinitely worse. Trash, debris of all kind, was scattered about. Directly across the river from the muddy spot on which he stood was a huge building, a factory, sending out smoke from two big stacks above and sending some dirty, steaming substance into the river from pipes below.

Snowy was standing in about two inches of water. He peered into it and saw only blackness. He looked into the mud along the edge of the water where life usually teemed. There was no sign of a living thing. He started to walk along the shore but when he lifted his foot he found it black with some oily, sticky substance. Snowy left.

The two men stood silently on the bank watching the lone white bird fly away. On up the river he went, mile after mile. Still there was no sign of any life except human. No swimming birds in the water, no waders or shorebirds along the banks, no diving birds flying overhead. All was empty, lonely.

Snowy was beginning to get desperate. Food, a roosting place, companionship. These, to him, were basic necessities. He must find them. But how? Where in a land that seemed dried up and lifeless?

He did all he could do; he kept on flying. At length he saw a patch of green. As he got closer he saw that it was back a little ways from the river, on a tributary, a little creek flowing into the mainstream. Here there was a small lake about a hundred feet across with grass and cattails along its banks and on a small island in the center. There were trees and shrubs growing back from the lake, and the water flowing out of it looked clean until it reached the river.

It seemed to be just what Snowy was looking for, except for one thing. All around this oasis were houses. People were walking along the shores of the lake. It was, in fact, a little town with a park. Snowy had never before ventured into an area surrounded so closely by people. But never before had he been so desperate.

He started to circle over the park, uncertain what to do, when he saw that there were a good many birds already there. Ducks of several different kinds were swimming in the lake. Near the island he caught sight of a white wading bird. His uncertainty vanished.

Down he came, landing in shallow water among some cattails as far from the people as possible and near the white bird he had seen. This turned out not to be another small egret but a little blue heron still in his white plumage, and like Snowy, a year-old wanderer. Actually there was another little blue of the same age with him that Snowy had not seen from the air. He was back in the reeds and, being ahead of the other in molting, was now mostly all blue except for a few remaining specks of white feathers.

They were an odd-looking trio and already were drawing attention. People had gathered along the shore, looking at them and pointing. Snowy, however, had other things to worry about, mainly food. The birds were in shallow water with a stand of cattails between them and the closest bank. As long as the people didn't get nearer, Snowy could tolerate them.

The other herons had stopped to note his arrival. They now paid him little attention and resumed their own feeding. Snowy started walking slowly. After the chilling experience of the dead bank of the river, he was happy now to see signs of life. Almost at once he snared a small frog. To this he added some tadpoles and a water beetle.

Out in the deeper water Snowy could see some minnows but they were wary. He waded out a little and stood stone-still. After a few minutes one of the little fish came within reach and was added to the meal. This was fine, clear water. When Snowy had to defecate, he was careful to walk ashore so as not to becloud his hunting area.

There remained the problem of roosting. Snowy was going to let the little blue herons solve that for him. Their requirements were the same as his. At home they all roosted together. Whether they liked it or not, these herons were going to have company for the night.

As it turned out they welcomed him. They, too, were vagrants trying to find a place in the scheme of things. There was little room in the ever-shrinking feeding, roosting, and breeding places for new generations. The old birds stayed. The young were forced out to wander in search of new places. Only a few would make it and these would often have to adapt themselves and change long-ingrained biological habits.

That was what these herons were doing. Their normal roosting place was in trees or bushes tall enough to render them as safe as possible from ground predators and with enough foliage to guard them against enemies in the sky. But these birds had been unable to find any such place that wasn't surrounded by people. So, when the sun started down, instead of flying off to a roost, the little blues simply went into the tallest and thickest part of the cattails. As Snowy watched, they started climbing, using feet, wings, and bill as Snowy had climbed around the mangroves before he could fly. They climbed about two-thirds of the way up and, grasping several of the largest cattails in each foot, managed to make a perch.

Snowy followed them into the reeds and made a similar ascent. It was by no means his steadiest perch, but he found if he grasped just the right number of cattails they bent down under his weight to an approximately horizontal position. At least he was not now alone, and he was perched over water. He bent his legs and let the tendons lock. His sleep that night was disturbed only fitfully by the unfamiliar man-made noises of the town.

For a while Snowy settled into the routine of life on the little lake. Food was not as plentiful as on the salt-water flats in the south, but competition was not as great. But the area was limited and often there was nothing to be found but the minnows, and they seemed to be getting ever more wary of the hungry birds. The little blues mostly stood and waited for this prey. Something in Snowy's genes told him there was a better way.

Once, when he was poised in hopeful waiting, he remembered the success he had had using his foot to stir mud or grass. He extended his leg and vibrated it gently just under the surface. The bright yellow of his toes flashed in the rippling water. A little fish, attracted by the color and motion, came to investigate. It was his last investigation.

Snowy also had some success using his bill and tongue as well as his yellow foot as a lure. Standing in shallow water, he would extend his neck out over the surface and submerge his bill, opening and closing it rapidly, or he might flick out his tongue to create little ripples. Minnows and other creatures would sometimes also come to investigate this. These methods by no means always worked, but Snowy would often get more food this way than the little blues did with their patient waiting.

The band around Snowy's left leg bothered him some in this. Although he did peck at it sometimes in preening, he was seldom aware of it otherwise except in this hunting. He disliked feeling the metal ring shake back and forth so he never used his left foot in stirring or as a lure. Even so, when he vibrated his foot, he could feel the ring on his other leg.

Snowy was learning many things in his new environment, and one day he learned an entirely new way to entice little fish within reach.

Some person on the shore was dropping pieces of bread into the water. One came floating toward the herons and Snowy could see little fish rising to eat of it. He waited, and when it got within striking distance he easily caught one of the minnows.

The bread floated out to deeper water, out of the herons' reach. But soon another piece came floating their way, and this time all three birds managed to get fish. They watched again, sadly, as the bread started to float away from them, the little fish going out of reach along with it. But some inspiration seized Snowy.

He waded out, grasped the bread in his beak, brought it back and placed it again in the shallower water. The minnows were lured in and again the birds got fish. Snowy repeated the process until the bread disappeared. It was another lesson, but one he was unlikely to benefit from very often.

X

Despite the apparently easy, safe life in the lake in the
park Snowy was restless. He longed for more companions, especially of his own kind. And he longed for wider
spaces with more variety in hunting. Yet he still remembered, with terror, the lifeless, foodless land he had passed
through before reaching this park. He wanted to leave,
to go elsewhere, but he was fearful.

He started watching the ducks who usually stayed by
themselves out in the deeper water. Many of them were
now leaving, small flocks taking off almost every day.
Snowy noticed that they always headed in precisely the
same direction, almost due south. Ducks had always

meant water. Snowy would follow the course they set.

So one morning after feeding he took off, circling high above the lake to avoid the town. His two companions, the little blue herons, were following. Snowy headed south in the direction he had seen the ducks taking.

All of his old fears began to come back. The land below looked much like that over which he had passed after leaving the drained-out marsh—towers and wires, houses and highways, brownness instead of greenness, rivers without grass, flats without life, air that stung the eyes.

But Snowy would not turn back. On he flew and soon the three birds saw what looked like green growth and clean water ahead of them. They increased their speed. Finally they arrived over it. What a sight!

Below were expanses of open water on which were hundreds of ducks and geese and diving birds. Along the shore were grassy flats and marshes on which count-less wading birds like themselves were feeding.

Gulls and terns were circling overhead and a few shorebirds ran along the banks. Beyond some wide dikes there was an expanse of tidal water in which were more birds. At various places were clusters of trees that of-fered safe roosts.

Snowy saw a large group of white birds. They were little egrets like himself. The companions he had longed for! He circled down and landed beside them.

Snowy had found his way into a large national wildlife refuge.

Life in the refuge was not quite as easy as it might have seemed. There were more birds here than normally would have occupied the same area, so the competition for food was keen. Also, it was a refuge for all, predator as well as prey. Many of Snowy's enemies were about.

There were also people. But there was never any threat from them. As in some of the places he had been in the south, the people, when they were present, simply stood on the dikes or moved along them gazing at the birds. All in all, the refuge was the best place by far that Snowy had found since leaving home. Here, for a time, he would be content.

As the summer progressed, all the herons began losing their gaudy plumage. Snowy's own plumes, shorter and less abundant than those of the older birds, began to drop away to be replaced by the plainer feathers he would wear until next spring.

He was, in fact, undergoing his first complete molt. Like almost all birds during this process, usually in late summer, Snowy felt less inclined to be active. He was quieter, less sociable, more often by himself, and spent a great deal of time concealed by reeds or other cover.

Gradually he would lose all his feathers, each being replaced by a new one. In preening now he carefully pecked at the budding sheaths, helping the new feathers to break out and grow. He felt some alarm when the first big wing feather fell off each wing, but there were always replacements before the next ones were lost. Thus Snowy was able to fly at all times during the molt, although not quite as agilely as at other times.

In this regard he was more fortunate than the ducks. Many of them were nesting in the area, back in the drier grassland, but, as soon as the egg laying started, most of the males, leaving all the work of setting and raising the young to their mates, returned to the ponds. Snowy often saw these drakes gathered together out in the water.

Their plumage was changing rapidly now. And, as would also happen to the females later, they had lost so many feathers from their wings that, for a time, they could not fly at all. When enemies appeared these ducks would either dive under the water or scurry for the shelter of grass or cattails. There was no escaping into the air.

And enemies did appear. One day Snowy was alerted by a warning from one of the older egrets. *Awrk! Awrk!* He looked up to see a big bird swooping down toward them. Snowy recognized the white head and tail —an old eagle. The herons sidled up beside some protective cattails. They were not overly alarmed at this bird, for he was not very adept at catching live prey. This was about to be demonstrated.

The eagle was not headed for the herons but for a flock of small, chunky ducks, brownish with white cheeks, out in the water. These were *Ruddy Ducks*. The male ruddy, unlike any of the other ducks, behaves like a goose in that he does help the female in raising the young. This job had been finished by now, and flightless birds of both sexes were in the flock. They had carelessly moved a little too far from protective covering. This had attracted the eagle.

Most of the ruddies scurried across the water to some sheltering reeds. But one was a little too far out to risk exposing himself that way.

Down came the eagle, eager talons extended. Just as he was about to strike, the ruddy dove. The eagle pulled in his talons, swished past, turned, and made ready for another attack.

Again the ruddy dove just as his pursuer was about to

strike. Again he was able to come up and get his air safely before the eagle could make his turn and come back. If this had gone on long enough, the ruddy might eventually have tired, failed to make his dive at just the right moment, and fallen prey to the eagle. But each time he dove, the duck swam closer to the cattails. He finally managed to get in among them, exhausted but safe. The eagle flew off disconsolately, still hungry.

There were other attackers from the sky, however, who were more efficient. Snowy had often watched some rather noisy, friendly birds the size of small ducks with drab, dark bodies and white bills. These were *Coots.* Snowy had seen them in the marshes in the south along with their close relatives, the red-faced *Gallinules,* and their more distant cousins, the shyer rails.

One afternoon a group of these coots, after feeding in the shallow waters, had come up on the shore of a little island to rest. Suddenly there was a fast-moving shadow —short, round wings and a long, thin tail.

Desperately the coots squawked their warning and struggled to get into the water. There they could dive for safety. The attacker was too swift. One of the coots was seized in vicious talons and borne away, squawking and struggling. It was a *Cooper's Hawk,* one of the most feared of the predators.

By the end of July, Snowy had completed his molting. He was now an adult bird, his plumage for the first time in every way similar to that of his elders. He found now that sometimes he could challenge successfully an older bird if one came too close to what he thought was his hunting territory. There would always be more as well as less dominant birds than he, but never again would he yield to another simply because he was younger.

By late summer there began to be some new arrivals among the herons. Some little egrets came in that, to Snowy, looked shabby and appeared to fly clumsily. These birds were three or four months old—the new generation, eternally seeking some place in their ever-shrinking world where they could find food and security.

They were not exactly welcomed by the older birds in the refuge. As Snowy had been the year before, they were forced to feed on the outer edges, in the least desirable places. In the roosts at night they were often forced almost to the ground where many fell victims to roving raccoons and foxes. Others had to perch so high they became prey for owls. Many of those who survived would move on, seeking other places. Only a few would manage to remain.

There was a great deal of restless movement among all the birds. From time to time flocks would leave and others would arrive. Individuals or pairs sometimes flew in or out, all for no apparent reason. Now, however, there began to be birds with more purpose in their movements.

For some time Snowy had noticed large flocks of the shorebirds he had known in the south, sandpipers and plovers, arriving in the refuge. They landed usually in the early morning, sometimes before dawn. They rested and fed along the banks. Sometimes they would stay a day or two, sometimes a week. But always, some evening, they would disappear and others would arrive to take their place.

These little birds were the long-range migrants who traveled by night and rested by day. Many came from breeding grounds far in the north and were headed for winter quarters far in the south.

Other birds, too, were starting to move south. In August, Snowy saw the first big flight of ducks heading out with definite purpose. These were *Blue-Winged Teal*, small, fast-flying ducks, the vanguard of a mass movement. Other ducks of many kinds were getting ready to leave, and flocks of the big Canada geese were arriving in the refuge on their way to the southland.

All of this filled Snowy with his own restlessness. He was not essentially a migrant. Many of his kind were those who nested in the north. If nothing else the weather forced them each year to seek hunting grounds in the south.

But Snowy had been hatched in the south. He had yielded to a vague migratory urge after his rejection at the nesting colony and had come north. Most of his fellow southerners, if they could manage it, stayed home or near it. That is where Snowy wanted to be now. His urge was not migratory but homing. It was no less strong.

Still, Snowy would not travel alone. He waited. With all the movement going on, it was not long before a little flock of egrets like himself took off. Snowy joined them.

The return was to be a leisurely one. There would be no long nonstop flight like that of the birds impelled by the breeding urge whom Snowy had joined for the trip north.

The present flock was being led by an unhurried old bird who seemed thoroughly familiar with the route. They had left after a morning feeding and flew by daylight. They passed over more of the world of men that Snowy had found so distasteful on his earlier travels. Soon they came to more open, greener country and could see wide bodies of water on either side. They were between the Atlantic Ocean and the Chesapeake Bay.

They came to more smoky air over buildings and houses and harbors filled with boats and men. Well beyond all this the leader brought them down. They landed on a thick stand of bushes and trees near an inland tidal flat. There were a good many other birds already roosting there but the newcomers found room, made short work of their preening, and fell asleep.

At dawn, hunger being the imperative demand, they were out on the flats. The hunting was good. They fed, rested, and fed again. None of the birds appeared in any hurry to leave; the weather was still warm and food was plentiful. For several days they hunted on the flats and in a swamp farther inland and roosted in the trees and bushes at night.

Then one morning after a feeding, the old bird who had led them here took to the air. Snowy, his restlessness never far submerged, flew up with him. Some new birds joined them and some of those who had come with them from the north. A good many of these stayed behind. They weren't ready yet to leave a place where food and shelter were available.

The new flock headed southwest, following the white line of the Atlantic beach. They did not exert themselves but a wind came up behind them and they made swift progress. After several hours the leader shifted their course inland until they came to a river. Here he turned again and followed the river upstream.

This was very different from the dead river Snowy had followed farther north. Here there was grass along the banks, trees hung with moss, and reeds and other vegetation in the shallows. When they came to a place where the river broadened out over some marshy flatlands, the flock came down.

They landed in shallow water. There was still an hour before sundown so they busily started hunting. Prey was not as plentiful as on the salt-water flats or in some of the marshes farther south, but Snowy managed to seize a good-sized frog and several water beetles before the flock went into some nearby trees to roost.

There wasn't a great deal of food here but there wasn't much competition either. They stayed by the river for some time, during which they saw only three or four other little herons, one great blue, and a kingfisher.

Snowy was particularly hungry for minnows, his favorite food. Often he could see the little fish, but always out in the deeper water beyond his reach. Unfortunately there were no mergansers or cormorants here to drive them inshore. He remembered getting fish while hovering in the air that day out in the gulf. He flew out over the school, but here there were no hungry big fish underneath to keep the little ones on the surface where birds could get them. At Snowy's approach they ducked down under some moss.

Snowy now combined two techniques, hovering and stirring. Maintaining himself in the air with his wings, he dangled a foot down and stirred the moss. A minnow darted out. Snowy managed to get him, striking from the air. With this success he would use this method quite often in the future when hunting was poor along the shore or in shallower water.

Fishing in the deeper water, it turned out, was not without its hazards. The next day, when Snowy was out on a log, he was joined by another member of the flock. The newcomer was careful to stay several feet away. Snowy, with a gesture of aggression with his neck and bill, let the other bird know he would not be tolerated any closer. With that tacit agreement the two stood, both motionlessly peering into the water, waiting for prey. Often an alarmed little fish would try to escape by heading straight down. It was then necessary to strike, with force and swiftness, quite deeply into the water.

Snowy heard a gurgled cry of pain from his companion. He looked over and saw the bird flopping helplessly, half on the log and half in the water. In a deep strike he had impaled himself through the eye on a twig hidden under the surface. Snowy flew off. He never fished from a log again. In the morning the bird's body was gone, a meal for some lucky predator.

After a week on the river, the birds awoke one morning shivering. The temperature had dropped several degrees. Once more they set off toward the south.

They flew over forests of small pine trees, farms and towns, an occasional river or swamp. That afternoon they came down where they saw some other birds feeding in one of the swamps. There was room for them so they fed and roosted with these birds, who were mostly Louisiana and little blue herons. In the morning they fed and took off. Many of them, like Snowy, were southerners and the falling temperature had given urgency to their desire to be home.

That afternoon they arrived over a large inland expanse of water, Lake Okeechobee. They crossed it and flew along the southern edge. Here there were miles of embankments, man-made dikes and canals full of dirty-looking water. All this made the lake shore itself uninviting but south of it there were wide fresh-water marshes with nearby roosting places. Here the birds came down.

This was home for many of them, but not for Snowy. He was a coastal bird. Home for him would always be where the salt water was. He fed and roosted with the flock that night but in the morning he flew off. Three other little egrets joined him.

Snowy needed no guidance now. With unfailing confidence he led the little flock into the west. After two hours they could see tidal flats in the distance and beyond them the broad sound where Snowy had started life.

They were hungry. Snowy wanted food before concluding the flight, so he started down toward one of the inland marshes where he had fed so often. Suddenly his confidence began to ebb. Where was the marsh?

Every instinct told Snowy this was the place. His memory could not fail. But there was no marsh! Instead there was a network of crisscrossing roads, towers and wires, a few houses being built. Soon it would be a drained and dry community where people could live, but not herons. Snowy could not change his world but others were changing it.

Snowy led the flock on. He could do nothing else. The birds came over the tidal flats and here there was change too.

In the mangroves along one side were two machines. Huge scoops reached out from them into the flats, digging up the mud and sand that was so full of life and dropping it, to dry and die along the edge of the lagoon. Land for men was being manufactured out of food for others.

Near the other side of the flats there were many birds. Snowy led his group down among them. With some difficulty and many shows of aggression, he established room. It was very crowded. Fully half the feeding ground was doomed.

XI

Snow was home although it was a home quite different from the one he had left.

Winter was coming on and many flights of birds were arriving daily from the north. There simply was not enough food or room for them. The younger birds, new arrivals and many of those whose home this was, and the less dominant older birds were forced to go on, to search elsewhere.

Snowy had no more than his share of dominance. But this was home for him. That gave him an advantage over those who had been hatched elsewhere. His urge to stay here was stronger. Although continually compelled to make warning displays, threats, or even, sometimes, actual attacks, Snowy managed to defend his chosen places at the hunting grounds and at the roost.

He settled into the old routines. The winter passed and soon the days were getting longer and warmer. The mysterious glandular changes began working again in Snowy's body. Now two years old and fully adult, the urges this released within him were stronger, the physical changes more pronounced.

Most noticeable, of course, was the new plumage. Old feathers dropped away from his head and neck and back. They were being replaced by long silky plumes that ended in wavy filaments. Now this prenuptial molt was bringing him plumes as magnificent as any other's.

Often he felt an overriding urge to show them off. It was a means of asserting his authority. He simply had to prove that he was more aggressive, more powerful than others. On the feeding flats or on the beaches he would display his new plumes to the fullest, warning others that he was the master.

He would seldom pick quarrels with the different companions on the feeding grounds, the other herons and ibis. For the most part they were more peace-loving anyway. But Snowy would often attack and try to drive away another bird of his own kind, even when his territorial rights were not being threatened, just as he had been driven away the year before.

He got into actual fights whenever the other bird stood his ground, which was quite often. He won some and lost some of these contests. Often the engagement would be broken off by mutual consent, a tie. After a little fighting the birds would suddenly lose their desire for further combat. Each would feel he had made his point. In all of it, nobody ever got hurt.

One day Snowy found himself headed for the Key. Quite a few birds of his and of other kinds already were there. The process of procreation was in its various stages.

Snowy circled about and landed on a mangrove branch five feet away from another little egret. *Aard! Aard!* This bird uttered his warning. He lunged at Snowy. Snowy cried out just as lustily. He lunged back. Above all else, he now felt the need for a place of his own, a place to be held and defended against all comers. And his present perch, halfway up in the mangrove very close to where he himself had been hatched, was going to be it.

Seeing that Snowy meant business, the other bird returned to his perch. The boundary line was drawn between the two territories, two and a half feet from each bird.

Now both of them felt compelled to tell the world: "This is my property." *Aard . . . ar-ogle! Aard . . . ar-ogle!* Each tried to outshout the other. Snowy felt supreme. This was his. Eagerly he advertised his ownership. Angrily he drove away any other bird who came too close.

He roosted on his newly won territory that night. In the morning, for almost the first time in his life, he felt no hunger. Instead he felt an increasing desire to continue announcing the fact that he was now a bird of property.

Bending his head back, pointing his bill upward, extending his new plumes to their fullest, he called out for all to hear and see. But whenever any bird came too close he would temporarily stop the display and drive him, or her, away. At the moment all he wanted was to assert his ownership.

After a while one bird, driven away two or three times, kept coming back. The urges within Snowy began to change. As he had seen in the displaying bird the year before now, in a matter of seconds, the yellow on Snowy's feet and on the bare skin between his beak and eyes turned bright coral-orange.

Instead of driving this bird away again he put on an even more striking display for her benefit, for now he recognized femaleness. He rose in the air, tumbled down, and landed beside her. She remained. He was accepted.

They began to caress each other with beaks and necks. They flew together in a little circle and came back to Snowy's property. There their first mating took place.

Both went to work diligently at nest-building. Snowy secured the sticks, sometimes fighting other birds for them, while his newly won partner wove them together. Snowy would present each stick to her with a courtly bow. Sometimes they would stop to caress each other and mate again. This would go on for several days, until the eggs were laid and the setting began.

Soon Snowy and his mate, who had undergone a similar change, lost the red coloring on their feet and in front of their eyes. Unlike the elegant long plumes that endured until the summer molt, the color changes came just at the height of courtship and lasted only a few days. In some other birds in the colony Snowy could see even more dramatic color changes. The bills of his friends the little blue herons turned a brilliant shiny blue, the pale yellow legs of the noisy black-crowned night herons became red, and the bills of the cattle egrets turned bright scarlet.

These distinctive changes, along with each step in the elaborate courtship rituals, served to prevent interbreeding, to preserve the species. For neither wooed nor wooer would undergo responses leading to successful mating unless procedures peculiar to its species were followed.

Snowy, like almost all the other males in the colony, had no desire for anyone else's hen. On a few occasions, especially among the little blue herons, he did see males stray over to other half-constructed nests when the hen was alone. Sometimes she would drive the intruder away, but sometimes she would submit. Such promiscuity, however, was the rare exception rather than the rule.

Snowy and his mate would take turns going to the feeding grounds. One always stood guard to see that sticks were not pilfered from their nest. And when the first egg was laid, setting or guarding was even more vigilant. For the fish crows were always above, a constant menace.

As soon as the first egg was laid, the birds took their turns at incubation. One egg was added each morning until there were four in all. Eighteen days after the first egg was laid, the oldest baby was hatched. The others came along, each a day later. With the hatchings, the real tribulations of parenthood began.

The presence of the babies, their *kek-kek-kek*, their seizure of his bill, all released within Snowy and his mate the overriding urge to bring them food.

Snowy soon found himself in a state of continuous exhaustion, not only from the constant trips to and from the feeding grounds but also from lack of nourishment for himself. Hungry and losing weight, the commands of parenthood nevertheless bade him disgorge the food from his own stomach and put it into those of his babies.

The problem was compounded by the shortage of food. With so much of the principal mud flats gone and the nearby fresh-water marsh drained, Snowy and his mate, try as they would, simply could not get enough food for the four hungry infants.

The youngest never got any at all. He soon died. The next youngest got little and was wasting away. Despite his pitiful cries and the desire of his parents to feed him, there was seldom anything left by the time the two older ones had been shaken off. Soon he died too.

For a time, by working themselves into a state of near collapse, Snowy and his mate managed to keep the two remaining youngsters alive. But both were constantly hungry, even more hungry than normal. Irritated and restless, the youngsters fought with each other much of the time.

Finally the older one killed his sister. She was too large to swallow and was pushed out of the nest. A vulture below, at least, benefited from this. Organic matter was never wasted in Snowy's world.

With only one hungry little stomach to feed, the parents now could manage. Their sole surviving offspring grew rapidly. Soon he was eating solid food and flapping his little wings.

Some timing mechanism within Snowy told him when the youngster should be forced to fly, when he should be taken to the nearby shallows and shown how to hunt for himself, and when he should be led to the general feeding grounds. All of this proceeded smoothly.

Snowy and his mate, once more able to eat and keep their food, now began to regain their lost weight. At the same time they began to lose their long, fluffy nuptial plumage. They also began to lose their attachment for their youngster and for each other.

The day inevitably came when they separated.

With his family duties for the year behind him, Snowy nevertheless stayed around his home area. As the summer gave way to fall, bringing an even greater influx of visitors from the north, the problem of getting food became more and more difficult. The roost at night became more and more crowded.

Snowy was now an old bird and one well established in the neighborhood. This gave him a great advantage in the struggle for survival. When large flocks were feeding on the tidal flats, he could have one of the more choice locations where the most food could be obtained. At night he was always near the safer center of the roosting tree. But still it wasn't easy.

At times, when tides had covered the flats or when there were too many birds there, he liked to search for new feeding places. He seldom did this alone now, for he had become something of a leader, and when he flew off anywhere a few other birds, mostly younger ones, usually joined him.

One day, as Snowy led a small flock over some inland fields, they saw a group of white birds in among some browsing cattle. Attracted by this—because where there are birds there usually is food—they came down.

When they had landed they saw that the birds were not of their kind. They were the shorter-necked cattle egrets, like the ones who had taken over the nest in which Snowy had been hatched after he had left it.

These birds, as they often did, were following the slowly grazing cattle, usually two birds to each animal. If another bird strayed near the occupied side of a cow, he would quickly be driven off. One-half a cow—two hoofs—was the jealously guarded feeding territory. Every now and then one of the hoofs would stir up a grasshopper, locust, or some other insect out of the grass. The bird on that side would pursue it.

There were some cows with no birds beside them and these spots were quickly taken by the newcomers. Snowy found he had the most success if he stationed himself just ahead of an approaching cow. Often he had to jump away quickly to avoid being hit by a huge bovine head or crushed by a heavy hoof, but he managed to catch several grasshoppers fleeing the same dangers.

After a while the cattle stopped feeding and lay down to rest in some shade. The birds of both kinds gathered nearby, resting and preening. In some bushes Snowy saw a flock of tiny birds with yellow patches on their wings, heads, and above their tails. They were *Myrtle Warblers*.

One of the cattle egrets had seen them too. He strode over to the bushes. The warblers hopped on through the leaves away from him. The little birds had stopped to rest after a long migration. They were tired and one of them was too slow. The cattle egret seized the struggling warbler and swallowed him much as he might have swallowed a large insect.

Occasionally, Snowy had seen larger egrets and great blue herons catch small birds as well as little mammals. But here was a heron no larger than himself getting this kind of prey. Snowy moved over to the bushes, but by this time the warblers had disappeared. He never would catch a bird. Now and then, if one got close enough, he might lunge at it, but the birds were always too quick for him.

The sight of the cattle egret swallowing the warbler had stimulated Snowy's hunger. The cows were still resting. Snowy took to the air, his little flock following. Instead of leading the flock away, he circled back and landed near the recumbent cattle. Squawking loudly, he made aggressive gestures toward the animals, even prodding one with his sharp bill. The cows, who probably were about to do so anyway, lumbered to their feet. They resumed grazing and Snowy and the other birds were able to feast on some more insects they scared up.

His home area offered a reasonable livelihood for an established bird like Snowy, but still his old restlessness often stirred within him. Nothing now urged him to go north. But something bade him move, bade him try other places.

He remembered the broad marshes he had stopped at so briefly the last night of his return journey from the north, the marshes near Lake Okeechobee. One day he set out, heading east. Three of the birds who often followed him on feeding trips joined him, now bound for wherever he might lead them.

He led them inland. For two hours they flew until they came over the lake shore. Turning south from the bare earthen embankments and muddy canals, they came down in some marshy lowlands. Quite a few birds of different kinds were here. Snowy had no trouble asserting enough authority to gain a suitable place, but the younger members of his flock were forced to less desirable spots.

Snowy stayed in and around this marsh for some time. Often, when hunting was poor in the water, he would wander into the dry fields nearby, seeking insects, lizards, or almost anything else that moved and was not too large for him to get down.

One day he encountered a huge, rumbling machine. There was a man atop it working levers, and a huge blade out front was pushing up quantities of grass and earth. Snowy remembered following other big, moving objects—the cows—in a similar environment. He started walking along beside the machine. Other birds joined him. Insects were leaping for safety as the blade pushed away their grassy hiding places. Snowy and the others caught many. For several days they fed this way, until the bulldozer had completed its work. After that there would never be food there again.

Snowy also discovered a new enemy in this region, although to him it was more of a nuisance than a threat. He was feeding along the edge of the water one day when he saw, on a nearby tree, some blackbirds with long, wide tails, birds almost as big as the fish crows Snowy knew so well. He had just seized a large frog. Two of the blackbirds flew over. They cried out hoarsely: *Chek! Chek! Chek!* They flew about Snowy's head trying to seize the frog struggling in his bill.

Snowy managed to get the amphibian down. Then he lunged at his harassers so fiercely that they never would bother him again. They were *Boat-Tailed Grackles*, and while the fear of Snowy's sharp bill made them leave him alone, the same was not true for some other birds.

Not far away were several of Snowy's distant cousins,

the glossy ibis. They were busy digging little crayfish out of holes in the mud. The long, downcurved bill of the ibis was ideal for this, and the birds were securing many victims. As the crows had discovered in the nesting colony, however, the bill of the ibis was not so efficient as a weapon. The grackles had discovered this too. Most of the crayfish pulled out of hiding by the ibis were being snatched away by these black robbers.

It was now late winter. There had been little rain and the marshes where Snowy liked chiefly to feed were shrinking. Again he felt a compulsion to move.

He remembered the miles of grassy marshes interspersed with clumps of roosting trees that he had passed over on his first travels, to and from Florida Bay. He had last seen the bay area and much of the grassland devastated by the hurricane. But much of it had remained unspoiled. Snowy headed south.

As usual, a few other birds joined him. They flew over dry grassland, cypress swamps that looked brown and arid, and came to the expanse of grassy lowlands. For several miles they flew over the Everglades until they came to a small, open pool of water near a stand of pine trees.

Snowy led his flock down. Then he saw that what had looked like water from the air was, in reality, mud, dry and cracked. He started to fly on when he saw that beyond the mud there was some water. He was hungry. He flew to the edge of the water and landed.

There were fish here, some quite large. But they were dead. And they had been dead too long to interest Snowy and his companions. Across what was left of the pond was a large alligator, also dead.

The birds did manage to find a few living creatures in the mud and water. Snowy, standing and waiting, saw a movement and struck. He came up with a twelve-inch water snake struggling in his bill.

Snowy had caught and eaten a good many baby snakes, especially baby moccasins, but he had never tried to handle anything this size.

The snake, twisting and squirming, wrapped himself around Snowy's neck. Snowy walked inland and tried to beat the reptile against the dry mud. He was too big to be subdued this way, but Snowy did manage to get his neck free.

He was hungry and was not going to give up this much food. Carefully shaking his head to keep the snake from getting wrapped around him again, he worked to get his bill over his victim's head. The snake resisted for all he was worth, again trying to get a hold on Snowy's neck. The struggle went on for half an hour. In the end it was the snake who tired first. Snowy got a grip on his head and, with some effort, gulped him down.

The birds roosted that night in the pines. They were awakened just before dawn by a noise they had never heard before. It was a fire sweeping through the dry grass and now about to engulf their trees. Birds and other animals, those who could, were fleeing in front of it. Snowy took off and this time did not stop until he had reached the salt water of Florida Bay.

He did not know it, of course, but the water that should have been here was being carried elsewhere in that network of dikes and canals he had seen along the shores of Lake Okeechobee. They were causing the Everglades to die of thirst.

The whole area had recovered now from the hurricane, from nature's devastation. It was doubtful that the area would ever recover fully from man's devastation.

Snowy stayed along the shore of Florida Bay through the rest of the winter, hunting in the tidal flats and roosting in the familiar mangroves.

Then came the longer, warmer days. Snowy's gaudy plumes began to grow again. The old urges stirred within him. He had to go home.

Without stopping he flew, leading a little flock, back to the area where he had started life. He fed on what was left of the flats and headed for the Key.

Many other birds were there. But instead of landing they were circling about in the air, above the little island. Snowy saw why. There were men on the Key, men with a big machine like those Snowy had seen on the flats.

They were digging up the sand and mud from the shallows where Snowy first had fed. They were making dry land over the roots of the mangroves where Snowy had courted and raised his young.

Like the other birds, for a little while Snowy flew about. He felt only bewilderment. All the urges of spring had left him. He flew away.

In the Patuxent Wildlife Refuge at Laurel, Maryland, not far from Washington, there is an office operated by the Bureau of Sports Fisheries and Wildlife. There the records of the movements of thousands of birds are maintained and studied.

In that office, one day later that spring, a man was preparing data for a machine. From a pile on his desk he was picking up little metal bands that had been around the legs of birds. Referring to his notes he was dictating into a microphone.

"Number 869 dash 62792," he said. "Leucophyox thula, Snowy egret. Banded by Fish and Wildlife agent as a nestling, Pine Island Sound, Florida. Recovered after bird shot by a poaching plume hunter, Lago de Maracaibo, Venezuela."

He started to reach for the next band, stopped and looked again at his notes.

"I wonder," he said to himself, "I wonder what he was doing way down there. At nesting time he's supposed to be home."

Bibliographical Note

A WORK of fiction does not, ordinarily, call for a bibliography. This is, of course, a work of fiction in which I have taken certain liberties for the sake of the story. But as far as the behavior of my subjects is concerned, I have tried to make every incident conform to scientific observations. Much of this is based on my own field work. But much is also based on the accounts of others. I would like to acknowledge my debt to them.

This book could not have been written without the help and encouragement of my wife, Jane Eads Bancroft, in the field, in hours of listening and in constructive criticisms. I am also grateful to others.

First I would like to express my appreciation to the lecturer and photographer Hal H. Harrison and his wife and fellow naturalist, Mada, for many fruitful hours of guidance in the field and for reading this manuscript and making helpful suggestions.

Valuable guidance in the field came also from Dr. Andrew J. Meyerriecks of the University of South Florida, whom I believe to be today's outstanding authority on American herons. His published accounts that, in addition to field work, were especially helpful include:

"Comparative Breeding Behavior of Four Species

of North American Herons," Nuttall Ornithological Club, Cambridge, Mass. (1960).

"Foot Stirring Behavior in Herons," *Wilson Bulletin*, Vol. LXXI (1959), 153–58, and (same title), *Auk*, Vol. LXXXIII (1966), 471–72.

"Diversity Typifies Heron Feeding," *Natural History*, Vol. LXXI (1962), 48–59.

"Plumes, Threats and White Beauty," *Natural History*, Vol. LXX (1961), 20–25.

"The Great White Heron" (with Robert Meyerriecks), *Natural History*, Vol. LXVII (1958), 52–56.

"Egrets Serve as Beaters for Belted Kingfisher" (with David W. Nellis), *Wilson Bulletin*, Vol. LXXIX (1967), 236–37.

Dr. Meyerriecks is also a major contributor to the comprehensive and valuable *Handbook of North American Birds* (Ralph S. Palmer, ed.), Vol. I, Yale University Press (1962).

Recent concentration in the field of ethology has, of course, added tremendously to our knowledge of bird behavior, and the amount of modern published material is overwhelming. But the work of earlier observers still has much to offer.

Like every student of bird life, I am forever indebted to the late Arthur Cleveland Bent for his monumental twenty-three-volume work on the life histories of North American birds. These were first published by the United States National Museum, Washington, D.C., starting in 1921, and have since been reissued by Dover Publications, Inc., New York. For the present book the most useful of Bent's works were his *Life Histories of*

North American Marsh Birds and his *Life Histories of North American Petrels, Pelicans and Their Allies.*

Another earlier ornithologist whose accounts are still timely and useful is Frank M. Chapman. I found much valuable material in his *Camps and Cruises of an Ornithologist,* New York, D. Appleton, 1908, and in his *"Home Life of the American Egret," Bird Lore,* Vol. X (1908), 59–68.

Another observer of that generation to whom I am indebted is E. A. McIllhenny, who, on his own property in Louisiana, maintained a large heronry and kept the birds under almost constant scrutiny. His works include: *Bird City,* Boston, Christopher, 1934, and *Autobiography of an Egret,* New York, Hastings House, 1939.

Other sources specifically helpful in the categories indicated include:

Courtship, Nesting, Infancy

Allen, Ted T. "Notes on the Breeding Behavior of the Anhinga," *Wilson Bulletin,* Vol. LXXIII (1961), 115–25.

Almond, W. E. "Display of the Cattle Egret," *British Birds,* Vol. XLVIII (1955), 433–34.

Bancroft, Griffing. "A Great White Heron in Great Blue Nesting Colony," *Auk,* Vol. LXXXVI (1969), 141–42.

Baynard, Oscar. "Home Life of the Glossy Ibis," *Wilson Bulletin,* Vol. XXV (1913), 103–17.

Cahn, Alvin R. "Louisiana Herons and Reddish Egrets at Home," *Natural History,* Vol. XXIII (1923), 471–85.

Cottrielle, William P. and Betty D. *Great Blue Heron*

Behavior at the Nest, Ann Arbor, University of Michigan Press, 1958.

Cruickshank, Helen. *Flight into Sunshine*. New York, The Macmillan Company, 1948.

Farmer, Donald S. "Control Systems in Bird Reproduction," *Natural History*, Vol. LXXVI (1966), 22–27.

Hotchkiss, C. Taylor. "Anhinga Courtship," *Everglades Natural History*, Vol. II (1954), 44–45.

Meanley, Brooke. "Nesting of the Water Turkey," *Wilson Bulletin*, Vol. LXVI (1954), 81–88.

———. "A Nesting Study of the Little Blue Heron," *Wilson Bulletin*, Vol. LXVII (1955), 85–99.

Noble, G. K., et al. "Social Behavior of the Black-Crowned Night Heron," *Auk*, Vol. LV (1938), 7–40, and Vol. LIX (1942), 205–24.

Scott, W. E. D. "Bird Rookeries of the Gulf Coast of Florida," *Auk*, Vol. IV (1887), 135–38.

Tinbergen, Niko. *The Herring Gull's World*. Revised edition. New York, Basic Books, 1960.

———. "Sexual Fighting," *Bird Banding*, Vol. VII (1936), 1–8.

U. S. Department of the Interior. "Waterfowl Tomorrow," Washington, Government Printing Office (1964).

Van Vleck, Sarita. *Growing Wings*. New York, Doubleday, 1963.

FEEDING BEHAVIOR

Buckley, P. A. and F. G. "Tongue Flicking by a Feeding Snowy Egret," *Auk*, Vol. LXXXV (1968), 678.

Christman, Gene M. "Some Interspecific Relations in the Feeding of Esturine Birds," *Condor*, Vol. LIX (1957), 343.

Cunningham, Richard L. "Predation on Birds by Cattle Egret," *Auk*, Vol. LXXXII (1965), 502–503.

Dawn, Walter. "Cattle Egrets Provoke Cattle . . . ," *Auk*, Vol. LXXVI (1959), 97–98.

Des Lauriers, James R. "Co-operative Feeding Behavior in the Red-Breasted Merganser," *Auk*, Vol. LXXII (1965), 639.

Dickenson, J. C., Jr. "Unusual Feeding Habits of Certain Herons," *Auk*, Vol. LXIV (1947), 306–307.

Lovell, Harvey B. "Baiting of Fish by Green Heron," *Wilson Bulletin*, Vol. LXX (1958), 280–81.

Parks, John M. and S. L. Bressler. "Joint Feeding Activities of Certain Fish-Eating Birds," *Auk*, Vol. LXXX (1963), 198–99.

Rice, Dale W. "Symbiotic Feeding of Snowy Egrets with Cattle Egrets," *Auk*, Vol. LXXI (1954), 472–73.

Sprunt, Alexander J. "An Unusual Feeding Habit of the Snowy Heron," *Auk*, Vol. LIII (1936), 203.

———. "Predation of Boat-Tailed Grackles on Feeding Glossy Ibis," *Auk*, Vol. LVIII (1941), 287–88.

General Behavior

Allen, Arthur A. "Stalking Birds with Color Camera," Washington, National Geographic Society (1963).

Allen, Robert Porter. "The Roseate Spoonbill," New York, National Audubon Society (1942), reissued, New York, Dover (1966).

Ardrey, Robert. *The Territorial Imperative.* New York, Atheneum, 1966.

Armstrong, E. A. *Bird Display and Behavior.* Revised edition, New York, Dover, 1965.

Brackbill, Henry. "Herons Leaving Water to Defecate," *Wilson Bulletin,* Vol. LXXVIII (1966), 316.

Howard, Eliot. *Territory in Bird Life.* London, Collins, 1920, and New York, Atheneum, 1964.

Lorenz, Konrad K. "The Companion in the Bird World," *Auk,* Vol. LIV (1937), 245–73.

Lowe, Frank A. *The Heron.* London, Collins, 1954.

Pearson, T. Gilbert. "The White Egrets," *Bird Lore,* Vol. XIV (1912), 62–69.

———. "Herons of the United States," *Bird Lore,* Vol. XXIV (1922), 306–14.

Tinbergen, Niko. *Bird Life.* London, Oxford University Press, 1954.

———. *Curious Naturalists.* New York, Basic Books, 1958.

Weigel, Robert D. "Unusual Death of a Common Egret," *Auk,* Vol. LXXIX (1962), 118.

Welty, Joel Carl. *The Life of Birds.* Philadelphia, Saunders, 1962.

Birds in Hurricanes

Christensen, Ernst T. "Betsy in the Everglades," *National Parks Magazine,* Vol. XXXIX (1965), 22.

Douglas, Marjory Stoneman. *Hurricane.* New York, Rinehart, 1958.

Lane, Marilyn. "Hurricane Donna Visits the Everglades," *National Parks Magazine,* Vol. XXXV (1961), 11–13.

Robertson, W. B., Jr. and H. B. Muller. "Wild Wind and Wild Life," *Audubon Magazine,* Vol. LXIII (1961), 308–11.

Sell, R. A. "Effects on Bird Life of the Corpus Christi Storm," *Condor,* Vol. XIX (1917), 43–46.

LIFE EXPECTANCY

Kahl, Philip M., Jr. "Mortality of the Common Egret," *Auk,* Vol. LXXX (1963), 295–300.

Owen, D. F. "Mortality of the Great Blue Heron . . . ," *Auk,* Vol. LXXVI (1959), 464–70.

BIRDS AND MEN

McHarg, Ian. "Blight or a Noble City?," *Audubon Magazine,* Vol. LXVIII (1966), 47–52.

Pennekamp, John D. "100 Years of Wasting Florida Water," *Audubon Magazine,* Vol. LXVI (1964), 46–47.

Schneider, William J. "Water and the Everglades," *Natural History,* Vol. LXXV (1966), 32–40.

Teale, Edwin Way. *North with the Spring,* New York, Dodd Mead (1951).

Trumbull, Stephen. "The River Spoilers," *Audubon Magazine,* Vol. LXVIII (1966), 102–10.

U. S. Department of the Interior. "Birds in Our Lives," Washington, Government Printing Office (1966).

Whitman, Leroy. "Restoring George Washington's River," *National Wildlife,* Vol. IV, No. 5 (1966), 3–9.